A Matter of Fear

A Matter of Fear

Seymour Shubin

Five Star • Waterville, Maine

Five Star First Edition Mystery Series.

Published in 2002 in conjunction with Tekno-Books and Ed Gorman.

Set in 11 pt. Plantin.

Printed in the United States on permanent paper.

Library of Congress Cataloging-in-Publication Data

Shubin, Seymour.
    A matter of fear / Seymour Shubin.
       p. cm. — (Five Star first edition mystery series)
    ISBN 0-7862-4310-4 (hc : alk. paper)
    1. Vanity presses — Fiction. 2. Pharmaceutical industry — Fiction. 3. Publishers and publishing — Fiction.
    I. Title. II. Series.
    PS3569.H754 M38 2002
    813'.54—dc21   2002023180

For Gloria
with love

Chapter One

I can't think of that building, even years later, without thinking of darkness. I felt it the first time I walked in there, though God knows it had enough windows and lights, and even though I hadn't as yet met any of the people, and the murder of course was still months away. And I still can't think of Samuel Wallace Glennie without the urge to shout at his memory that with just a few words he might have saved himself.

It was only after he was gone, that euphemism for dead, that I became fully aware of how little I knew of him. And this was even before the first suspicion stirred that this quiet, lumbering man had been murdered, bringing with it every question of his past and present. I simply knew nothing about him, compared to what I *came* to know, though we had worked together for about five months.

He was always Mr. Glennie to me. In fact it was only after he was dead that I began thinking of him as Sam, which sounds strange, I know, but which I hope I'll be able to explain. It wasn't that I was afraid of him or had all that much respect for him, not only as my immediate boss but as someone a lot older than I was: fifty-seven (I learned his exact age later) to my twenty-eight. Christ, I didn't have *any* respect for him. The truth is, I looked on him as something of a pathetic weasel. Sometimes, I swear, I wanted to hit him. Full fist.

But then again I felt like hitting a lot of people in that goddamn place, though not for the same reason.

Mallory & Mallory. Publishers since 1902. Mostly medical texts, though they had a small fiction and non-fiction department on the top floor, their trade department. And though I didn't know it at the time I entered their dark door, they were going downhill, a Mallory in a first-floor office still in charge.

All right, "dark door" is just an expression. But the whole exterior of the building, let alone the interior, gave off a sense of darkness. And enclosed within its massive, gray-stone four stories, and bay windows, was a kind of Dickensian fossil, with just about everything in thick walnut and its offices behind smoked glass. Though I have forgotten offhand that this was the time of the Watergate hearings (I've looked it up) and the year of Roe v. Wade, and which songs were popular then, I can still never forget, among so many things there, the heavy feel of the place each morning I walked in.

I was in the bathroom when the call came, and I wasn't able to get to it before the fourth ring. I don't think I finished my hello before this snarly voice broke in, "You looking for a job or not?"

"I am yes, yes of course."

There was a long pause, as though he were deciding whether to hang up. Then, begrudgingly, "Frederick Meehan. Mallory and Mallory. You wrote to us."

"Yes." My heart lurched. And I mean lurched. I'd been looking for a job for months.

"If you're interested, be here tomorrow. At eleven."

"Sure. Thanks so much—"

But he'd already hung up.

I remember looking at the phone, wanting to dial Information to give me that number, then calling that bastard and telling him—But it was three months that I'd been out of work, and a few hundred letters and resumés had gotten me maybe three interviews at most, after which I would stand again at the elevators that had brought me up, while all around me people were walking back and forth to offices and desks.

I'd worked for the past five years at Packer-Hill Laboratories, the pharmaceutical company. In their general promotion department, which included writing brochures and handouts and scripts for audiovisuals, some speeches for executives, and, not incidentally, thinking up gifts to give to doctors and their ladies at conventions. But then the patent on one of their biggies ran out, and some nine hundred of us were let go, though leaving a sizable population behind.

I must tell the truth: I had enough of my severance pay left that I wasn't looking for just any kind of work. Just editorial. A magazine, newspaper, book publishing, advertising agency, p.r. I hit New York, of course, and most of the major cities on the east coast, though not Buffalo where I had come from and where my folks still lived; it just felt like a defeat to have to go back there. But then came this, whatever the hell "this" was.

My first sight of Frederick Meehan was of this thin, red-grayish-haired man of about fifty-five, waiting for me in the open doorway of his office at the far end of an office-lined area that was filled in its center with desks and cubicles. He wore a tight, drab, brown suit, complete with vest. His face, which I came to think of later as a ferret's, was sallow, his glasses, through which stern eyes stared, frameless. He was, though I didn't know his full title then, editor-in-chief of the medical division and a vice-president of the company.

He sort of grunted as I came close—at least it looked from the movement of his mouth like a grunt, for it was silent—and then he turned and sat at his desk and looked down at some papers while I stood there awkwardly. I took a chair. And it was only then that I noticed this other man sitting in a corner. He was hefty, balding, sloppy-looking, his tie pulled a little to the side.

Meehan kept looking at what I assumed was my letter and resumé, then raised his head long enough to say, "Glennie," with a nod at him, his introduction, and "Loberg," with a nod at me. "That's . . . Thomas, right?" he said, after another look down. Then he leaned back and looked at me. It seemed to be mostly at my hair, which suddenly felt a little too long for here.

"We really don't have an opening."

I felt a sagging inside me, wanted to leap across the desk at that scrawny throat. But then I knew it was either some kind of ploy or plain and simple wickedness. That other guy wouldn't be in here otherwise.

"What we have here," he went on in a clipped way, though it was a while before I realized he was mostly looking at the far edge of his desk, "is a separate section of our medical division. Special Projects. We put out medical books under our regular colophon that we couldn't ordinarily afford to publish. Not enough of a market. Require special financing."

In other words, I caught on quickly, vanity publishing. An island in the center of this venerable old company.

"If we do make an opening," he was saying, "it's for someone who'll help Glennie here with acquiring titles, reading, editing, production. Salary? I don't know. But couldn't be what Packer-Hill pays. We're not a drug company."

No, indeed. The salary he finally mentioned was little more than half of what I'd made.

The only thing else I remember him saying was to repeat that at this moment they didn't have an opening, but "we'll see." Mr. Glennie said nothing though with my instigating it we did shake hands before I left. I didn't even try with Meehan. Nor did he.

I walked down the aisle, past the other offices, then didn't wait for the elevator to go down the three flights to the first floor. I opened the front door to spring air that was clean and bright. I loosened my tie and took off my jacket. I was anxious to get back to my apartment, to get into shorts and go for a run. But I couldn't wait. I broke into a run, on center city sidewalks. But it wasn't as though I was running to something. But away.

I should have kept running.

Chapter Two

Four days later Frederick Meehan called me. No hello.

"Loberg?" It was almost a growl.

"Yes."

"You still looking for a job?"

I wanted to say, "No, you prick." I said, "Yes."

"Then be here Monday. At nine."

I looked at the phone a long time after putting it down. I had this quavery feeling of dread. I had convinced myself, after two days of not hearing, that I would never hear, and with it had come a feeling of thank God. But not completely. I didn't have to stand on my toes to see the end of my severance pay. And along with that I'd begun to think of book publishing as something I'd really like to get into.

So this job, as lousy as it might be, could be my entry, something important on my resume. Something to use.

I'd left Brown a major in English Lit, with no concrete plan how to use it and, since I'm not out to kid anyone, went for my masters because it was a deferment from the army and Viet Nam. Then afterward, as I pretty much just waited, the draft people didn't bother me, and, well, I didn't bother them. I got a job in the advertising department—a fancy word for two desks in a corner—of a freaky alternative paper, then went into writing for it. The paper died a year later, and after several months I got, through a friend of a friend, an interview at Packer-Hill. And there, almost despite myself and my wonder how anyone could exist in that bright, clean,

12

ultra-modern atmosphere, I got the job, largely because my interviewer had gone to Brown, I know. There I joined, on the lowest rung, a department of some fifteen writers. I still think of my first day, sitting in my L-unit, called that because, yes, it was shaped like an L, when I heard the tinkle of a bell and peered out, and there was this coffee wagon, and toward it swarmed the inhabitants of the offices and L-units, where they would stand around talking until drifting away ten minutes later. I literally got vertigo in the midst of sipping my coffee, and had to hold on, as though nonchalantly, to the open door of an office.

I never thought I would be staying there long, but somehow I was good at the work, and came to like the idea of such things as cost-of-living raises, which had nothing to do with your actual, periodic raises, and flying first-class and even helping research scientists write papers in basic, readable English. And I liked most of the people in the department I worked in, almost all of them good writers with an interesting history or a story: it was almost us against the rest of the suits in the company. And so when, sitting in my unit, I heard the first stories about Woodstock that began to drift out, it was with a touch of envy but no real regret.

One of the things I'd come out of Packer-Hill with was a background in medicine that was almost infinitely less than people assumed: I'd had a lot of inhouse experts and texts to turn to in helping me say some nice words about just a few products. So to bolster my severance pay, I called a publication in New York that I'd heard was looking for freelance medical writers. It was a magazine for family physicians, a freebie, a throwaway, that was thick with ads. When the editor heard my background, he was happy to give me an assignment: write an article based on a telephone interview of an MD/PhD who had some thoughts on treating choanal atresia. There were two things wrong with it as far as I was concerned. I didn't know what choanal meant, and I didn't know what atresia meant.

But I found a *Dorland's Illustrated Medical Dictionary* at the library (choanal, pertaining in this case to "the paired openings between the nasal cavity and the nasopharynx"; atresia, "absence or closure of") and with a kind of band around my heart called the doctor. I told him right off how little I knew about the subject, that I might be asking him some dumb questions, but that he would see the article to make any changes before publication. And he agreed. And it worked out well enough that I got another assignment. But the magazine folded by the time I finished it—and no other one wanted it. Or me.

I went out for lunch shortly after getting the call from Meehan. Although I had a fairly nice setup for a studio apartment, with a pullman-kitchen behind folding doors along one wall of the living room-bedroom, I wasn't big on making elaborate meals for myself.

The building itself was small for an apartment house, five stories with a marble entranceway and a pretentious pillar on each side. The area, a little south of center city, was predominately a well-to-do one, though many of its large, stone row houses had been converted into apartments and doctors' offices. It was only about six or seven miles, along almost a straight line, to the house of Mallory & Mallory. My apartment was on the first floor, close enough to the elevator to hear it, and too close to everyone else to smoke pot freely, which I never did much anyway, or alone.

I went to the corner drugstore, Silverman's, which had a counter and several tables where they served breakfast, lunch and dinner. Sid, and sometimes his wife, was always wishing me a good Hanukkah or Passover, whatever, obviously assuming from my name I was Jewish: they never questioned it and so I never told them. I was sort of used to it in fact; even got a perverse kick out of it, and don't remember correcting anyone, including a couple of kids in grammar school (no, one was in high school) who called me a kike.

Silverman's was fairly crowded, as usual for lunch, but there was an empty seat at the counter. I ordered a sandwich, an egg salad as I remember, and since there was no room to open the newspaper I'd brought along, I looked absently in the long mirror behind the cash register at the faces at the counter. This one girl stood out. She had long glossy black hair, parted sharply in the middle, falling to each side of a slender face that was smiling, under a perfect nose, at someone next to her. And she wasn't wearing a wedding or engagement ring.

She was still sitting there with someone, a much older woman, when I left. I looked at her long enough to see she was wearing a tan pants suit, the jacket open to a white blouse, the bottoms a little flared as was the custom. She was just lighting a cigarette.

Outside I wondered, as I'd been wondering, who she was—someone who'd just moved in or had just started to work around here, or a patient or other transient I would never see again?

I started to head back to my apartment but changed my mind. It was too beautiful a day. I had three more days before I walked into the joy of Mallory & Mallory, and already I couldn't get enough of the sun. But actually I felt a lot better about the whole thing. I'd stay there as long as I felt I was getting something out of it for the future, and even if it turned bad right away no one could keep me there.

I walked down the quiet one-way street on which I lived to

a small park, a square block of greenery just off the major business streets. It was always busy when the weather was good, but with room for a lot more. Mothers and babies. People on benches eating their lunch. Lovers.

But though there were many pretty girls, I was still thinking of that face, that body, at the counter.

Chapter Three

Since no one told me where to go I reported to Meehan's office from the elevator but he wasn't there. A few moments later a gray-haired woman who looked to be in her late fifties approached me. "Mr. Loberg?"

"Yes."

"I'm Mrs. Dwyer, Doris Dwyer," she said with a smile. "Mr. Glennie's secretary. And yours."

While people looked at me from their desks, I followed her to a cubicle which I was to learn was a few feet from Mr. Glennie's office. It was spare, with a phone, an electric typewriter on a metal table, and some basic supplies on the walnut-colored metal desk. The desk chair was a swivel, the one other chair a hardback.

"Can I get you something?"

"No. No, thank you."

"Would you like to look at my newspaper? I always buy one to bring home to my husband."

"No," I said for no reason. "But thanks."

"Well, I'll be right out here if you need me."

I watched as she went to her desk, where she was in full view to Mr. Glennie and me. I sat back and looked around. There was nothing on the walls or, except for a *Webster's Dictionary*, on the single shelf. I will hang pictures of Queen Victoria and her court, I thought, though someone else here has probably already done it.

I wondered who'd worked in this cubicle before. Apparently, from what Meehan said, no one had held this job. I began opening drawers, wondering if he or she had left anything behind, perhaps a warning. Bare.

I sat there, just looking out at whoever was walking the aisle. Mrs. Dwyer came in soon to ask again if there was anything she could do for me.

"No, really. Thanks. Oh, who worked in here before?"

"The editor of a journal we used to publish. A very nice woman." Then she said in a whisper, "It didn't do well."

Mr. Glennie showed up after a while, holding several books. "Thomas?" That was his hello.

"Good morning."

"Here's a few books we've published. Give you an idea what we do. There's a lot more in my office. Come in and take any of them when you're finished."

The books he left behind, mostly slender hardcovers, included a history of a mental hospital on its 100th anniversary; an anesthesiologist's experiences during the Korean War; papers presented at a seminar on rheumatology; a book of short poems called *Patients Mine: Verses of Affection*, by a family doctor. I glanced at some of the poems, now and then pausing to read.

The Secret Door

You think you don't know me; really know
Me.
Look into yourself and you will know me. All people,
it's become almost trite to say, are really
One.
You are part of my life as I am part of yours.

I closed the book, gathered up the others and went into his office. He looked up from his desk long enough to point to the space on the shelf where they belonged, and said again I could take whichever of the others I wanted. I scanned the spines slowly, occasionally pulling one out. There were the published papers of seminars; other collections of poems, a couple by nurse practitioners; monographs by MDs and osteopaths; something called *Jesus and Your Dog*, by a veterinarian; *If Freud Played Ball*, a psychoanalysis of oldtime baseball players such as Cobb, Matthewson, Lefty Grove—

"Thomas." I knew who it was by the voice, and when I turned Meehan had already passed my back and was standing next to Mr. Glennie. I said, "Good morning."

He turned slightly. "Morning," then immediately looked back at Mr. Glennie. "Look at this," he said, putting down an illustrated page proof. "Cropped it all wrong! God, man, you should have learned this in the third grade!"

I quickly swung back to the books. He left almost immediately. When I turned to go, I saw in a fast, embarrassed glance that Mr. Glennie looked perfectly fine as he studied the page. Not even a touch of red on his cheeks, or gray where the blood might have drained away.

I went back to my cubicle. I hated that little bastard more than ever—just let him try that on me. But my anger wasn't only at Meehan. It was also boiling at Mr. Glennie, for taking it.

Mrs. Dwyer obviously felt sorry, or awkward, for me, since no one else came around to see me that morning. She brought me a medical dictionary, and a little later a *Roget's Thesaurus* and a *Manual of Style* from the University of Chicago Press, after which she just stood by the front of my desk, as if trying to decide whether to say something. When it came out, it was: "You know, you look a little like my son. I mean the black hair. Of course he's much older—he's thirty-eight now, and you're a little taller. My husband used to have real black hair but he never wore it long. He wore a buzz. He was a motor-cycle cop, you know."

"Really?"

"But he had a heart attack and he's been on retirement ever since."

"How is he?"

"Good. Just can't exert himself too much."

"How long have you been working here?"

"Twenty-two years. But not all in this department. I came over here when Mr. Glennie came. That was fourteen years ago." The fingertips of one hand on my desk, she stood poised there, as if ready to take off. But then she said, in a quiet voice and after a little look around, "We used to be much busier here. It's fallen down quite a bit."

"Is that so?"

"Yes. I don't understand why."

I reflected on it a moment, immediately wondering why the hell then had I been hired. "Which floor's the trade department on?"

"The fourth," pointing toward the ceiling. "They've also come down quite a bit. They used to be in New York. This company," she said with a solemn shake of her head.

A few minutes after she left, a figure appeared in my doorway. It was a man of about forty, with a lot of uncombed blond hair and big teeth. He was grinning.

"So," he said, "you work for him."

Just that. I stared at him.

"Has he taken you up on a UFO?"

I didn't have time to say anything, for right after that he was gone. I sauntered out as he was disappearing into one of the far offices.

"Who's that?" I asked Mrs. Dwyer.

20

"Mr. Roper." She made a slight face. "He's right under Mr. Meehan. He's an acquisition editor."

"Lovely fellow. I must invite him to dinner."

And not long after that I could see people gathering in the aisles to go out to lunch. They began drifting past us. No one came over to me, nor to Mr. Glennie. When I walked into the doorway of his office, he was holding a book a little in the air while he was absently opening the wrapper of a sandwich on his desk. I could see it was Camus' *The Stranger.*

"I'll be going out," I said.

He looked up just long enough to nod. I stood there a moment longer, wondering what the hell Roper had been referring to about UFOs.

I walked over to join the flow down the aisle. I was a little surprised to see Meehan standing outside his office with Troy Roper and another editor—and he was actually smiling, though thinly. I'd never seen him do even that before. No one as much as glanced at me. Or maybe that's not fair. Maybe two or three of the secretaries did. But it didn't take long for me to realize that everyone, Meehan included, looked on us in vanity as pariahs.

When I came back from lunch I delayed a little getting off at the third floor just to see who was staying on for the fourth.

I wondered how the hell I could get to be a trade editor.

Meehan saw me coming down the aisle, and he started walking toward me in a crab-like way, one shoulder forward as though threading through a narrow path. He came with me into my cubicle, where he dropped a large-sized, cardboard box of manuscript and photos on my desk.

"Might as well get your feet wet," he said in his clipped, growly way. "Came through regular medical. No good, not for us but could be for Special. Look it over but damn it don't

21

spend your whole life reading it. Call the doctor, say it's good but we need help publishing. Say it's not our regular audience and we don't know what kind of market it'll be."

"Okay."

"And don't offend him, for God's sake. Frokin's chief of medicine down there in Tampa."

"What if he agrees? What kind of money do I tell him we're talking about?"

"That's not your worry." He looked annoyed that I would even bring it up. "Tell him I'll be in touch with him."

I sat down with it at my desk. It was a thick manuscript, close to four hundred pages, complete with cardboard-backed photographs, called: *World War II Medicine: The Back Line on the Front Too.* I glanced at several pages, saw that it was a history of a base hospital in England, with as much emphasis on naming all the medical personnel as well as the types of wounds they handled, and even each member of the USO who had passed through. I was turning a page when Mr. Glennie showed up in the doorway.

"Uh . . ." He hesitated. "What did Mr. Meehan bring?"

I lifted several of the pages. He came over and took them from me, began skimming through them, then gathered up the whole thing.

"I'll do this. I want you to do some proofreading."

I watched him lumber out, to return shortly with a handful of proofs. He set them on the desk, then left without a word. *You poor son of a bitch,* I remember thinking, *afraid I'm out for your job. If you only knew I wouldn't take it even if they threw roses in front of me.*

Chapter Four

I stopped at Sid Silverman's drugstore on the way home. Several people were there, a couple of them having dinner, others with prescriptions or just standing in conversation by the newspaper and paperback racks. One was a girl I'd taken out about two months ago, but who had since become engaged. We greeted each other pleasantly; there was no pain on either of our parts.

The black-haired girl, the only reason I had come in, wasn't there.

I bought a pack of Life Savers from Sid. He said, "How's the new job going?"

"Not bad."

"Oh, if you ever want to publish a good book just spend a day here. It'll be an instant bestseller."

"I don't think my nerves could handle the excitement here."

"I'm telling you," he said.

I walked back out into the sun. Only advertisements were waiting for me in my vestibule mail box. I carried the crap back into my apartment and turned on the window air conditioner, which always rattled a little before settling down. Tomorrow seemed a long way off. And I had an attitude prepared for it. I remembered my father telling me a little story about the Depression, probably a joke but what the hell it served the same point. There was a run on a bank and everyone was standing in line desperate to pull out their money. But while everyone was moaning and groaning, this one lady was humming a tune. And when someone asked her why she was so happy, her answer was, "I'm only here for a calendar."

That's all the hell this job was going to mean to me.

Shortly after I got in the office I saw that Mrs. Dwyer was mailing back Dr. Frokin's manuscript. I felt fire go through me. Mr. Glennie had probably read the goddamn thing in maybe an hour yesterday, and had been turned down in the time it takes to make a short phone call. I was angry that he'd stolen it from me.

I couldn't have done worse, and chances were I could have done better. A few minutes later I went into his office. I wasn't there to quarrel.

"Do you have a few minutes?"

He nodded.

"Look, if I act naive about this it's because I am naive. But I was just thinking of ways of acquiring manuscripts. This one's so obvious I'm sure you thought of it. Do you ever advertise for manuscripts in the medical journals?"

He shook his head. "It's a good idea but the company wouldn't go for it. It's too obvious for us. Most of the trade don't know we're doing this, though God knows they may be doing it themselves."

"Then how about going to conventions and seminars and we see what we could stir up?"

"That's a perfectly good idea but if it's any distance away the company won't pay for it. No, we've got to do it where we are. World of mouth. See who's publishing in the journals. See where seminars are being held and contacting them about their papers. See what hospital is having a big anniversary. That sort of thing."

I stood there, trying to decide what else to say. I felt I might be mistaken but I sensed that he'd warmed up a little to me. But I wasn't mistaken. What he said next, however, was strange, right out of the sky. He said, "Do you collect anything?"

"Collect?"

"You know, collect things."

"Oh. Well, stamps, but that was years ago. And that was the last."

"I like to collect first editions." He opened his top left drawer and took out the Camus. He handed it to me, though for a moment I was hesitant about taking it. He nodded take it. I held it and looked at it and then gave it back. But there was a difference in how he held it. He rubbed it gently; seemed to feel it through his very skin.

"I remember," he said, "I was visiting this woman in Nebraska. She didn't let a lot of people on her ranch, but I called her and she must have thought I sounded decent. And she let me come up to the house, right on through—there must have been a hundred and fifty people standing way out on the road—and before anything else she showed me where it hovered over the field. I—"

"Hovered?"

"I—Where the UFO . . ." Then his face reddened. "I'm sorry." He smiled weakly. "I lost my train of thought."

But I wasn't about to let go. "You mean you went way out to Nebraska to see where it landed?"

"Oh yes, oh yes, my wife and I . . ." But he didn't finish. "Anyway. The point is I was in her house and I happened to see she had this first edition of *Leaves of Grass*. Way out in Nebraska. And you know what? After I admired it she actually gave it to me."

"Really? That was very kind of her."

"It really was. Oh well."

And that was it. Conversation over. What I wasn't to learn until later when they would come to gather up his things and clean out his desk, was that he kept a map of the United States in his drawer, with ink-drawn stars and arrows indicating every UFO site he and his wife had ever visited.

As soon as I came back from lunch Mrs. Dwyer came into my cubicle and whispered that two people were waiting for Mr. Glennie in his office but he wouldn't be back from the dentist for another hour. They'd showed up without an appointment, saying they wanted to discuss a book project.

"Would you talk to them?"

"Why not?"

They were a fat couple, probably in their early fifties; the husband introduced himself as Mr. Winston but I noticed that he didn't introduce his wife. She seemed to be suffering. I don't think she ever looked at me.

"I have the subject of a very powerful book," he said. "It will bring down the whole Episcopal church in this city."

I wanted to say, "That's really not the business we're in," but he jumped into my thoughts by saying to his wife, "Honey, now don't be embarrassed. None of this was really your fault. Remember that, honey." Then to me: "I happened to overhear this on the phone, when my wife was talking to her girlfriend. I wouldn't have known about it otherwise. But the two of them were in a bar when they met these two priests. This one priest started talking to them first—Is that how it started, honey?"

She nodded, clumsily.

"So this one priest started talking to them. I mean, who would suspect what was on the man's mind? And what happened then?" he asked his wife. "They bought you a couple drinks, and what? Asked if you'd go shopping with them?"

She nodded her heavy head again.

"This could be a tremendous exposé," the man said to me. "I want to bring this whole thing down. I want to tell everything. And then what happened, honey? Whose house did they stop at? I'm not all that clear on that."

"I don't know whose."

"You don't know, honey?"

"No, I'm all mixed up."

"They didn't say where it was, honey? Honey," he scolded her, "you're acting embarrassed. Remember, they took advantage of you. First of all, Pauline's a slut. I've told you. But you and your faith in people. And there was that whole atmosphere there. The drinks. You didn't know what you were doing. And you're human, you—you got worked up."

"Excuse me. Mr. Winston," I interrupted. "Hold on a second. Hold on. Let me understand something. Who referred you here?"

"You mean here to this office?"

"Yes, what brought you to Mr. Glennie?"

"I called here, I talked to people, I finally talked to someone, I said I had this sensational idea for a book. And they said come right up here."

"Did you tell them what it was about?"

"A little, yes. But I still haven't begun to tell you."

"I don't understand. We're medical publishers. We publish medical books. This is not our type of book."

"I don't care what kind you publish, this will be a great book. A big seller, it was two men of the cloth taking advantage of two women."

"I'm sure it'll be a terrific one, but it's really not for us."

"Not for you?"

"I'm afraid not. I'm very sorry."

It took me at least fifteen minutes more to convince him to stand up with her and leave. I watched them walk down the aisle toward the elevator. Then my stare drifted around the entire floor, settling on the blond head of Troy Roper. He was standing chatting and smiling at his secretary at her desk, facing this way though not looking at me. I would bet anything . . . Anything.

But Christ, I thought as I kept staring at him, Mr. Glennie wouldn't let himself get mad anyway.

Chapter Five

I saw the black-haired girl in Silverman's the next morning when I stopped in to buy a paper on my way to work. She was drinking a cup of coffee at the counter, her fine legs crossed, a cigarette between her fingers as she chatted with Sid. I thought of her for a long part of my walk through the early sun. Mostly, that she was out of my league. Even a little older, at least a couple of years, which in my mind was part of being out of my league. Troy Roper was among the few people clustered at the elevator. His face under his shock of blond hair broke into a grin when he saw me, and he held it as we got out and walked together down the aisle.

"I hear," he said, "you worked for Packer-Hill. This must be quite a change. No more all of those drug company perks."

I shrugged. "How much money can one person put away?"

He seemed to like that. "By the way." He'd stopped where I was to cut off to my cubicle. "Did you know a guy there named Ginsburg? At least I think it was Parker-Hill. A researcher."

I said nothing.

"He proposed a book for me, but it was terrible. And the son of a bitch wanted a mint."

I shook my head sadly and started walking away. "That, I'm afraid, is Uncle Ginsburg."

As I'd thought, Mr. Glennie didn't show much reaction to

the incident of the Winstons. He barely shrugged, and dismissed it with a little wave of his hand. I wondered what the hell ever bothered him.

Although I was sure as ever that he was afraid I was after his job, he now went out of his way to act as if we were simply colleagues. I put it to him being too gentlemanly not to. In that first week he gave me a list of doctors to contact about possible manuscripts; he turned a manuscript over to me for editing, though he handled the production anyway; laying out the pages, choosing print sizes, weight of paper, what kind of binding, that sort of thing. None of it interested me; we should have had the help of Mallory & Mallory's regular graphic arts department. But this was Frederick Meehan's way of having so-called Special Projects make a profit on very few salaries.

I asked Mrs. Dwyer if Mr. Glennie had any children and she said he had two daughters, teenagers. That week I saw a woman go into his office, and for no obvious reason I had the feeling she was his wife. When the two of them left together, I was sure I must have been wrong; otherwise he would have introduced us, wouldn't he? No. The woman, Mrs. Dwyer told me at her desk, was indeed Mrs. Glennie. I tried to gather together fragments of an image. I recalled her as about fifty, squarely-built, plain.

The only time I did see Mr. Glennie upset that week was when a shipment of books came from the printer, with the index pages bound into the heart of the text.

"My fault, my fault," he kept muttering to himself, although it wasn't his fault in any way. And then, to me, with a soft moan of despair: "What do you expect from someone who invests in a spaceship?"

I looked at him, startled, but he quickly averted his eyes, was looking back at a copy of the book as if somehow he could lift that index and put it in its proper place. But then he raised his eyes again.

"That's just an expression, of course. But I've done things just as crazy, so I might as well have invested in that."

But, again, it wouldn't be until later that it would become clear. And I would remember how hard he'd looked at me as he said it, how his eyes tried to convince me he was telling the truth.

The strange thing is that this time in the drugstore I didn't notice her. Not that it was crowded—there were maybe only four or five people in the place. I had a date for early dinner and had to pick up shaving cream and a few other things.

I saw her looking at me when I was standing at the counter. She smiled.

"Hi."

"Hello." I could feel my heart take a quick beat.

"When you're finished I'd like to talk to you if you have a minute."

I came over to where she was sitting at the counter. Looking up she said, "Sid tells me you're an editor with Mallory and Mallory."

"That's right."

"Well, I may be talking out of turn but you're someone my boss might like to meet. Dr. Crestman? Harvey Crestman? We're right around the corner—three-thirty-four. He's a cardiologist. I know he's been talking with publishers."

"Oh?" Nothing could have sounded dumber.

"He's quite a guy," Sid spoke up from behind the counter. "In fact he was just in here. He brought up something about a book and we were talking. I even mentioned your name, Junior. I said, 'Hey, do I know this editor. Worked with Hemingway.' I'm kiddin' but I did mention you."

31

"I appreciate this," I said to both of them.

"Do you have a card?" she asked.

Fortunately I'd just gotten them from the printer: Thomas Loberg, Assistant Manager, Special Projects. She looked at it, then held out her hand. "I'm Tina."

"Hi."

"I'll give this to him," she said, smiling, holding the card near her face.

"It's very kind of you."

What I didn't say—there seemed to be no reason to—was that his name was quite familiar to me. I had never met him but I knew his name from my former job at Packer-Hill Labs. He was one of a handful of doctors particularly high on the company gift list, all of them brilliant with high reputations, who though they might not do anything outright wrong, you could absolutely depend on when you needed a favorable paper or review or speaker.

Docs who some of us referred to as the company whores.

Chapter Six

She called me the next morning at the office.

"Tom, this is Tina Savoris. From the drugstore?"

"Oh." I was suddenly sitting a lot straighter in my chair. "Good morning."

"Look, I'm afraid I did talk out of turn," she said, her voice distressed. "I'm calling to let you know not to expect the book."

"Oh, I'm sorry."

"I'm very sorry. And I'm embarrassed."

"Please don't be. Why should you be embarrassed?"

"Well, I am." She suddenly seemed anxious to go. "It's one of those things. It wasn't my place to say anything."

"Hey, I'm not all that sorry about the book, I'm sorry you sound upset. That really bothers me."

"Well . . . that's all right."

And then without a goodbye, or one that I heard, she was gone. I sat there a while with the phone still in my hand. I set it down and kept it down for maybe ten minutes, then picked it up with a sudden urgency and called Information. Dr. Crestman had a few listings, his residence in the suburbs, a hospital, and his office in center city. The female voice that answered in center city wasn't Tina's, but she put her on.

"Tina, this is Tom again. Tom Loberg. I hate to bother you at work."

"You're not bothering me."

"I'd like to talk to you. And I was wondering if I could

33

meet you after work. Maybe we could have a drink?"

"Oh . . . That's very kind of you. But I don't know."

"Can I call you back?"

"Let me think. Things get so crazy around here. I'll tell you what. Let me call you."

I had the strong feeling she wouldn't go. And then when she did call, around three, I was in the men's room. But Mrs. Dwyer was holding her hand over the mouthpiece and looking at me as I walked up the aisle. She was smiling slightly. It's, her lips said silently, a young lady.

I swept up the phone in my cubicle. "Hello."

"Tom, Tina. That would be fine. Would five-thirty be all right?"

"It wouldn't be all right, it would be great."

She asked where to meet, and I suggested a little bar I went to now and then, The Weepy Dawg, which was several blocks from her office and my apartment. I got there a few minutes before she did. She was wearing a flowing, ankle-length flowered gown and flats. Her long hair glistened as though it were wet. She slid onto the stool I'd saved for her and immediately took out a pack of Kools. I shook my head when she offered me one, but I struck the match for her.

She ordered a Molson, I ordered a Harp. I said, "I'm so glad you could make it."

"Oh, I really needed this today. Did I need this."

"It was that good, huh?"

"It was that bad. God, were we busy. But they're all pretty busy."

I looked at her as her eyes drifted away for a few moments. Her irises had a touch of purple to them. She seemed younger than I'd originally thought, though I was sure she was at least thirty. She looked back at me and smiled, sadly it seemed.

"I'm awfully sorry. And I'm still a little embarrassed."

"About the book? No. Don't be. Anyway, maybe I've got this wrong. Didn't Sid say the doctor was in the drugstore and they were talking about his book and my name came up? Or did I hear wrong?"

"No, you heard right."

"Well, then what's the big problem about your mentioning it to me? I don't get it."

"I don't know. I told him about it and he just got terribly annoyed."

"Well, this calls for no higher than Psychology 101. It's his damn ego. He wants people to think publishers are flocking to him. He doesn't want anyone to know his employees are peddling it for him."

"I don't know." But she sounded as if she were about to defend him.

"Do you have any idea what the book's about? I assume it's on cardiology."

"Well, yes and no . . . I've seen parts of it and it's a little hard to explain. He's published a textbook, but this isn't a textbook. It's more a series of like essays. About patients, his practice, about various kinds of strange cures he's seen. One or two were published in a Presbyterian magazine. I think one was in some medical journal."

I really hadn't been all that disappointed about losing his book until then. But all at once it had become the kind of thing Special Projects was looking for. Something that must have bounced around like a rubber ball.

The growing noise in the place, where we could just about hear each other talk, drove us out after about a half hour. Standing out on the sidewalk, I said, "How about something to eat?"

"No, I don't think so. I'm really not very hungry. I think I'll head home."

"Ah, but you said very hungry. I'm not necessarily talking 'very.' "

She laughed. "Then what are you talking about?"

"Good question. People have been asking me that for years. There's a nice little Italian place—"

"You're going to think I'm terrible, but I had Italian for lunch."

"Yes, that wasn't very nice at all. Let's see, let's see."

It wasn't until, after naming a couple of other places, I mentioned a plain little hamburger joint and ice cream bar a few streets away that she nodded with a big smile. Sitting at one of the little glass tables, we each ordered a sandwich and a milkshake.

She started to sip on the straw when she quickly backed off and said, "I never thought about it. How does this go with beer?"

"It's the only way I drink milk."

"Seriously."

"Well, give this experiment five minutes. Check your watch. If I'm still around . . ." Watching her, I took a slow sip, then another. "You know something? It's terrific. I can still taste the beer."

She laughed, then cautiously took a sip, then not cautiously at all between bites of the hamburger.

"So tell me," I said, "what do you do in Crestman's office?"

"Just about everything except what I've been trained for. Mostly, that is."

"You really do that. I would never have guessed."

She laughed, then became serious. "I'm an RN but I've pretty much given it up, though once in a while I do help with a patient."

"Can I ask why you gave it up?"

36

"Sure. I guess I haven't been in it long enough to say I burned out but that's just about what happened. I went into the worst kind of cancer care—children—and I found it hard to handle. I would have stayed on, I felt so guilty about wanting to leave, but I met Dr. Crestman, he was visiting the child of one of his nieces. Somehow we got talking alone and I just began crying. And he told me he was looking for more office help and if I could type and would just help around I could do it for a while or until I was ready to go back into nursing. Whatever. And that's how it happened."

"And you're happy there?"

"For the time being anyway. But I'm ready to go back into nursing . . . It's funny," she said then, reflectively, "how your parents' attitudes can get to you. When I told them I wanted to go to nursing school, my father in particular was against it, though he finally did let me go. But maybe that's some of the reason I had a problem with it."

"What was his problem with it?"

"I know it had to do with my—you won't believe this—seeing naked bodies." She smiled. "Men's bodies. He would say it to my mother in Greek, like I didn't understand."

"What did he want you to do?"

"Get married. To another Greek. And work in his pizza parlor. In any order."

"Well, I'll tell you," I said, smiling, "there's something to a good pizza . . ."

She leaned across the table and hit me on the arm. "Now tell me about you. You must love publishing books."

She lived in the north section of the city, and generally traveled back and forth to work by bus. At first she didn't want me to drive her home but then gradually gave in and walked with me to the public garage where I kept my car, a Ford Pinto hardback. Once when I stopped at a red light I put my arm around her and she came toward me a little, only to tighten up and look at me with a tense little smile. I immediately withdrew my arm, as if I'd really been doing something more. I felt in that moment a lot more than a couple of years younger than she. And so much more awkward.

It was still gray with evening light when I drew up to her house, in the middle of a block of brick row homes with high front steps and small plots of grass. I started to get out but her hand tightened on my arm. "No, you don't have to. This will be fine."

"Am I allowed to watch you from here?"

"You're funny, you know that?" She kissed me quickly on the cheek. "Thanks so much for dinner."

"Oh, I must admit I really went all out."

"I enjoyed it. And thank you."

I watched as she walked up the steps to the front door. The door opened just as she got there, as though someone had been peering through a little opening in the closed drapes. And a woman stepped out, thin and pointy featured, who I was sure, from the way her head was thrust forward and her mouth was moving, was fiercely angry at her.

Chapter Seven

I found that once you initiated it Mrs. Dwyer was happy to talk about people in the firm, though with an almost inaudible voice and a frequent darting of her eyes. And so the next day when I asked in my cubicle if she'd ever seen Mr. Meehan smile, she went on to say, though ignoring that, what a brain he was.

"He can tell you the title of just about every medical book ever published, and who wrote it. I've seen him do it. Just ask him a question some day. Ask him."

"Forgive me if I don't."

"And he's something in his church. I understand he was a Catholic but he's been a Methodist for years now. And he's quite a family man. He and his wife have four married daughters."

Which meant, I couldn't help thinking, he'd had to screw at least four times in his life. I didn't want to picture it.

Mrs. Dwyer was about to say something else when my phone rang. She gestured to ask if she should take it, but I lifted the receiver.

"This is Tom Loberg."

"Mr. Loberg," a man's voice said, "this is Dr. Crestman. Harvey Crestman. I'm a cardiologist here in the city. Chief at Maynard."

It happened just like that. It had been over, and now all at once it wasn't. In fact, bizarrely, he was calling almost the exact time Tina had called yesterday to give me the news

I would see no book.

"Yes, hello Dr. Crestman."

"I want to talk to you about a new manuscript of mine. But first I want you to know I've published a textbook, I've had chapters in several others and have published well over a hundred papers. I would include my bio of course with the manuscript. That's if we agree I should send it to you. But I'm just mentioning it now."

"I understand." I quickly decided against mentioning, at least for now, that I knew of him from Packer-Hill.

"This one's quite different and I must say I'm very proud of it. More literary, if I may. I call it tentatively *Ways to the Heart*, which is really a play on words. I've written a series of essays about cases I've been part of, in which various factors have had a profound effect on the outcome—love, faith, finding one's biological parent, the use of nurses from one's own ethnic background, things like that. Not that I neglect the medical. But at the same time I'm avoiding the term holistic—it's too sciencey-sounding for this particular book. Which isn't a long book, by the way, but I think it's a powerful one."

"I would love to see it. I look forward to reading it."

"Well, I want you to know that if I do send it to you, you'll be having the first look."

"Good." Although that was baloney, since it would have been natural for him to go first to whoever had published his textbook.

"Miss Savoris in my office mentioned you," he said, almost as an afterthought. "I understand we're neighbors."

"Yes, I live right around the corner from your office."

"So, are you interested in seeing it?"

"I certainly am."

He didn't say anything for several moments, as though he

were considering this. "All right," he said slowly, "I'll send you the manuscript today. By messenger. I imagine you want it to come to your office, not your home."

"Yes. And I'll be back to you as quickly as I can."

It was a call that stayed in my head for a long while, as if he hadn't really hung up. I wondered what had changed since yesterday. From his voice, which was stern, almost brusque, I had the feeling he was one of those control freaks, that somehow this wiped away that Tina had taken the first hard steps in finding us for him.

I finished his manuscript at home that evening. He was right in that it was short; powerful, not at all, though it was sort of readable. It struck me that he had made a deliberate effort to write something popular that was both in and out of his specialty. And though I really had no way of knowing if it was something Mallory & Mallory would publish without a subsidy, I doubted it, like Never.

I'd wondered ever since I got his call if Tina knew about his change of mind. I was tempted to call her throughout the day, and even more when I came home, but held off until after I finished the manuscript. I got her home number from Information and dialed it quickly. A woman answered; her mother I guessed.

"Is Tina there, please?"

"No." Almost angry.

"Do you expect her home soon?"

"I don't know nothing."

"Can I call her later?"

But she'd silently hung up.

I wasn't going to call back that night or any other night, but about an hour later I was dialing her number again. And this time she answered.

"Tina, this is Tom. How are you?"

"Oh. Tom. Fine. How are you?"

"Good. Is it too late to call?" It was going on ten.

"No. No."

"I just want you to know I had a great time yesterday. I hope you did. And I hope we can repeat it. Is there any chance of seeing you some time this week?"

"This week?" Weakly.

"Well, whenever."

"I—No, this week is bad. I'm terribly sorry."

"There's nothing to be sorry about. I'll call you again, okay?"

"Sure. Sure."

My eyes watched my hand lower the receiver to the hook. All I could think of was: what a strange house.

The following day I gave Mr. Glennie the manuscript. And he was back to me with it the morning after that.

"It's something for us," he said, without enthusiasm. "How well do you know him?"

"I only spoke with him that once. When he called. But I knew of him from Packer-Hill. He does some things for them. At least he did."

"Well, call him, see what he says."

He dropped the manuscript on my desk and started to leave.

"Mr. Glennie."

He turned.

"What do I tell him? I still don't know anything about the money part of it."

"You're not up to that yet. When you are, Mr. Meehan will handle it. Just feel him out. Good luck."

I stared after him. Great, this was great. I didn't move for a few minutes. Then I reached for the phone book.

I wondered if Tina would be the one to answer. But no.

"I'm sorry," the woman who answered said, "but Dr. Crestman isn't here now. May I have him call you back?"

"Yes, please."

It was almost four when I got the call.

"Loberg," he said when he heard my hello. "Dr. Crestman."

"Yes, Dr. Crestman, thanks for calling. I did tell you I would get back to you quickly. And I've read it and my boss has read it, and we're both agreed that it's very good. But the thing is," I added quickly, "it doesn't fit into any of our regular category of medical books."

I paused and there was only silence.

"But it does fit into what we're looking for in Special Projects," I went on uneasily. "These are books that are published under the regular Mallory and Mallory colophon, are handled and distributed in our usual way, but they—require cooperative publishing. Special funding. We—"

"Wait. Stop. You mean, they have to be financed."

"Yes, because we don't see a large enough market for it. If it was a straight medical text, that of course would be different. But this falls between the cracks of categories—"

"Wait, wait, hold on. I don't have time for this crap, I don't want to hear any more. If you don't want it"—his voice was growing louder—"just send it back! You think you're the only house around? I've been published by Saunders, by Lippincott, by—I've been published by the biggest medical houses! I don't want to hear any more! Just send it the hell back!"

And so it was on its way to the mailroom within a half hour. But then several days later it was as though this whole conversation had never taken place.

★ ★ ★ ★ ★

The call came as I was flipping through one of several manuscripts the regular medical department had rejected, with good reasons.

"Is this Mr. Loberg?" The voice was so subdued it was moments before I recognized it. "Crestman here. Dr. Crestman."

I said, still caught up in the jolt of surprise, "Yes, Doctor, how are you?"

"Fine, thank you." That same quiet tone. "Look, you'll excuse me but I'm in a bit of a rush now. But I want you to know that I'm very gratified that you people like my book. Very gratified. And that Mallory and Mallory will be committed to it. I'm right about that, aren't I?"

"You certainly are." Was he kidding? I couldn't believe how the guy had put his hatred of us, his bellowing, right out of his thinking.

"And my title. Do you like my title?"

"Oh yes," though I could barely remember it. I could only think, What brought this on? What the hell was this about?

"Good," he said. "Good. Now tell me. When can we discuss a contract?"

Chapter Eight

I turned it over to Mr. Glennie, who turned it over to Meehan, who as far as I knew had never read anything of the manuscript other than the short report I'd written. The next I heard of it was the following day when Meehan, after walking quickly down the aisle in that shoulder-forward way of his, stood in my cubicle in that same brown suit, a little note pad in hand.

"That Dr. Crestman," he said to me, as though it were painful to say, and then read from the pad, "forty thousand copies," after which he nodded quickly. After waiting for this to sink in, he nodded again, which I was learning was roughly his equivalent of the Congressional Medal of Honor, then without a word left and went to Mr. Glennie's office, where I could see him standing in the doorway.

Leaning a little to one side to get a better view, I watched him reading from the pad, then abruptly walking away. And with that I first became aware that Mr. Glennie had been out of the negotiations too. And though I was almost having a brain orgasm about the size of the sale—5000 copies would have been a lot—and Mr. Glennie had to be happy about it too, I wondered if my having brought it in made him feel even more insecure about his job.

In the coming days Meehan himself began showing signs of changing toward me, though you would have needed a microscope to detect them. He began, for instance, to nod or grunt good morning to me. And he started coming into my cubicle to mention a news item or with a report or journal that might lead to books. Mr. Glennie, meanwhile, quietly took over the entire editing and production of the Crestman book.

I first became aware of this when I accidentally met Dr. Crestman's wife in Mr. Glennie's office. I'd walked in to give him something, and this woman was sitting by his desk. He seemed a little flustered all at once, and he said, "Thomas, I'd like you to meet Mrs. Crestman."

She was a tall, skinny blonde in her early fifties, who smiled a lot but with thin, dry lips. She'd come in, he explained, to discuss print, the book jacket, and the quality of the paper—for one thing, it had to be acid free. Mrs. Crestman, he went on, had been an art history major.

I know she came in several times after that, though I didn't talk to her again. Despite her smile she seemed to be, from my one take of her, a woman always on edge. And I was right. It was easy to see that Mr. Glennie had come to dread her: she was forever changing and re-changing her mind. And even outside his office you could hear her voice talking of her husband in a trilling, admiring way—"My husband. The doctor."

One day Mr. Glennie called to me as I was walking by his office. He was holding up a glossy black and white shot she'd just left with him of Harvey Crestman for the jacket.

"Thought you'd like to see what he looks like."

I took the picture, wondering if I would recognize him as someone I'd seen at Packer-Hill. I didn't. The doctor had, as I held it first at one angle and then another, something of Mussolini about his face—bald, stern.

In the meantime I hadn't seen Tina again, either in the drugstore or out walking in the neighborhood. And I didn't intend calling her anymore. First, she obviously didn't want to see me. And there was something weird going on there, with the mother. Still, I would always walk into Silverman's with a sense of anticipation, and would often deliberately walk past Crestman's office, which took up a three-story stone row house, hoping the front door would open and she would come out.

My social life was neither great nor bad. I was seeing one girl, mostly, who wore her hair fluffed out like a pyramid, which I didn't like at all, but she was as little pressure on me as I was on her. She was still as intense on rock concerts and disco as I'd been at seventeen, eighteen, but we also had some things in common, including sex without commitment. One day, while we were taking an otherwise beautiful ride in the country, she said, even as we were sharing a joint, "My mother asked me to ask how much you make a year." So I knew this was coming to an end, which happened to be about the time I met Tina again.

As it happened, I wasn't looking for her. I was walking along one of center city's shopping streets when I heard "Tom" and there she was coming across the intersection and waving to me. She was wearing a short, shapeless dress this time, which somehow looked shapely on her, with a very long Aztec-looking shoulder bag. And sunglasses. It was a bright Saturday afternoon.

We embraced briefly.

I said, "It's good seeing you," and she said, "It's good seeing you too. How are you?"

"Good."

"I don't see you in the drugstore anymore."

"You just don't look. I keep waving to you."

She laughed. "Oh, I thought it was someone warning me to go away."

I laughed with her. "Which way you heading?"

"Actually home. To the bus. I did a little shopping. Or rather returning some things."

"Did you have lunch?"

"Yes."

"Well, how about a cup of coffee?"

She looked at me. Then she smiled. "That would be nice."

We went to a coffee house I was familiar with on a nearby side street. It was fairly dark, its tiny empty stage and forlorn mike giving it the look of a shuttered theater, and empty except for a couple of young fellows at one of the tables and a girl in a half-apron standing resting on her elbows by the coffee urns. Tina took off her sunglasses and set them next to her.

I said, "Would you rather go someplace quiet?"

She smiled. "It is noisy, isn't it?"

"Sorry, but you'll have to talk louder."

We laughed together, then looked up at the girl who'd come over. We ordered regular coffees, black.

"How's your work going?" she asked.

"It's moving along okay. I don't know if you know it or not, but your boss changed his mind, we are publishing his book."

"Yes, I heard. I don't know what the problem was. All I knew was that he was going to publish it with someone else, and then I heard, just about accidentally, that you were publishing it. I can tell you this—he's very happy about it."

From my sense of Crestman, I was sure he hadn't told anyone in his office that he was subsidizing the thing. And I wasn't going to be the one to break the news to her.

"So," she said, "tell me something about yourself. I really don't know anything other than that you're an editor at this distinguished publishing house."

48

Oh boy. I said, "Well, to begin with I was the only child of abused parents."

"Now that's a twist. But come on." She tapped my forearm. "I want to hear."

"Well, I am an only child. I'm from Buffalo. It snows a lot there. Both my parents work for the same real estate company. I majored in English Lit, which was a way of trying to decide what I wanted to do. I worked for a so-called alternative paper, then got a job in promotion at a drug company, Packer-Hill. I was laid off with a lot of other people, unless they were lying to make me feel better, and voila. I'm at Mallory and Mallory."

"Are you happy there?"

"Oh, you're supposed to be happy?"

"Come on. Serious."

"Seriously, I think I've found the work I want to do. It's not exactly it right now, but I'm learning."

"Good." She said it softly, frowning. She suddenly looked troubled.

I said, "And tell me about your family."

It took a long moment before she came out of it. "Oh," she said, "I have two older sisters, much older, both married, both have children. My mother's sort of sickly. To be honest with you, she's a depressive. But it's nothing you put people away for, at least not for a long time. And that's, frankly, why I'm still living at home."

"Have you always lived there?"

"No, when I was going to nursing school I lived at school, of course. And afterward I lived with another girl, another nurse, for a few years. And then two things sort of coincided —nursing, you know, got a little much for me, and my mother got worse. So I moved back home. Actually, though, I'm looking for a place now."

"That sounds like a good idea."

"But it's not easy. You don't know Greek parents with their daughters. At least these."

We sipped at our coffee. Then I glanced at my watch.

"Look, it's not quite three. And it is dark in here and it's very light outside. If you're in no hurry to go back, I'm sure we can do better than this. Like take a little drive."

She looked at me. Then she picked up her sunglasses and nodded determinately. "Good idea."

I got my car from the garage. The tank was almost empty, which wasn't the best news during those times of the OPEC embargo, which meant gasoline shortages and long lines at the pumps and skyrocketed prices. But I'm giving it more thought now than I gave it then. In fact I barely gave it a thought, I was so caught up in the excitement of just being with her.

I headed straight out to the great horse farms that began about thirty miles from the city, drove slowly through the many one-lane roads, where horses peered over the fences or galloped in the distance or stood arched over nibbling the grass. We stopped at a couple of barn sales, bought nothing, which didn't seem to offend anyone, then had dinner at a Swiss chalet-looking place where we watched the evening slowly cloud the windows.

When we drove back and she saw I was nearing my garage, she put her hand on my arm and said, "Tom, no, please. Just take me home." And though I felt a rush of disappointment I was also aware that for the past half hour or so I had become quite anxious, as though this would be a first time for me. I looked at her, and she was pleading with me with her eyes, and her hand didn't leave my arm until I drove on.

"Thanks. I'm sorry."

"There's nothing to be sorry about."

It was black out, except for the glow of street lights, when I pulled onto her street. Cars took up all the parking spots near her house. I started to double-park, but she said, "No, park."

When I did and turned off the motor, she was sitting angled toward me. As I put my arms around her, her arms came around me, fiercely. Her cheek went against mine, then after several moments our mouths met, open, and my hands were against the back of her head, and hers were digging at my back.

It was only when I looked at her that I saw tears in her eyes. I said, "Tina."

She said, "Shh. No. Don't." She kissed me again, lightly this time. "Walk me up to my door."

I walked with her down the street and up the steps, and waited as she searched her bag for her keys. She suddenly seemed a little frantic, as though the front door might fly open. But she found them, smiled, silently said goodnight, and disappeared inside.

As I walked down the steps I felt a heaviness around my heart. I told myself to stay away from her, that she had troubles I didn't need. But I sensed that I wouldn't. And of course I was right.

Chapter Nine

A detective was to ask me had I noticed anything different about Mr. Glennie, and when. But I didn't need him to ask me, I asked it of myself before he ever came to question me. And of course there were things, signs. But none that was really a placard to what was going on inside him; none so obvious (at least I like to think) to prevent the horror. And who could have guessed at it?

The one thing all of us, the whole floor, were to think of immediately was his smoking. I had never seen him smoke, didn't know whether he ever had; but this one day, glancing into his office, I saw him hunched over his desk, a cigarette burning in one hand as he was measuring something with what looked to be his pica ruler. I didn't think much of it: those were the days long before no-smoking regulations began popping up in work- and public-places, the smokers consigned, if at all, to stand like cattle outside their buildings for brief breaks. Didn't think much of it, that is, until I heard him coughing, a raspy cough, throughout much of the day. And then late that afternoon Mrs. Dwyer came into my office to set down some office memoranda, and looked in his general direction and mouthed, puzzled, "Not in years." So I did wonder, but then after a few days he began cutting down to just a few a day, and I simply thought: it's his business.

And then there was that strange question.

I'm at my desk doing something or other when I sensed, or maybe heard in almost a subliminal way, a presence. And I looked up and there he is standing in the doorway, his left hand up on the jamb. His moon-ish face looked pink.

"I'm sorry to bother you," he said hesitantly, "but did you hear from anyone?"

My face must have registered What the hell're you talking about?

"I mean"—he looked to be in a whirl of confusion—"from her? From Mrs. Crestman?"

"No."

"Oh. I'm sorry. I thought maybe."

And then he was gone.

I stared at the emptiness he'd just left. What the hell was that all about? And then it seemed obvious. He'd taken over the Crestman book so completely, he was so jealous of it and worried about me, that he was afraid of my suddenly having any further part of it.

But the way he was acting, I could only think, was so stupid, so apparent.

Well, stupid maybe. But apparent, as I would find out, no. The fact, however, was that I had become too occupied with other things to spend much time analyzing him.

For one thing, I'd made a couple of sales. Small ones, in that each was about 2500 copies, but sales. And both came from my following up leads in the medical literature that came across my desk. I got the rights to publish the papers presented at a symposium on asthma, which would be paid for by one of the professional societies. Another was a thin book of tributes a private mental hospital was sponsoring as a memorial to a former chief of psychiatry.

And then there was the change that Wilfred Mallory III made in my work life.

Wilfred Mallory III was the last of the Mallorys actively involved in the old firm. The only times I'd ever seen him was from a distance, a tall, pencil-straight man in his early sixties, known as a breeder of a type of carriage horse seen only at certain high society fairs. He suddenly appeared in my cubicle a few days after Mr. Glennie had asked me that strange question about hearing from Mrs. Crestman.

"I hope I'm not breaking in at a wrong time."

That was the first I even knew Wilfred Mallory was in my cubicle. I sprang up from my chair.

"I just wanted to say hello."

"Hi." I could feel my heart going.

"And I want to congratulate you on your fine work."

"Thank you." I didn't know that anyone had passed along word. It couldn't have been Mr. Glennie. Meehan? *Meehan?*

He wasn't leaving yet. "Is this your first work in publishing?"

"In book publishing, yes. I was with a pharmaceutical firm, Packer-Hill. I was in their general promotion department."

"Good. Well, I'm glad we have you."

"I'm glad to be here." Almost leaving my mouth was: But I'd like to get into Trade. Not smart.

"Well, if you have any questions, any problem, let me know."

"Thank you. I will."

He reached out his hand. I shook it, hoping he didn't mind sweat. And now he was gone.

I sank back in the chair. No more than a minute later Mrs. Dwyer was in the doorway. She looked at me, incredulously. Then she said, her voice low, "He didn't go anywhere else on the floor."

"Really?"

"Nowhere. I'm telling you."

And then a few minutes after she left, she was followed by Troy Roper.

"Well," he said, letting out a breath between a weak grin.

"Well, what?"

"Well, what? Well, what?"

A few days later Roper even asked me out for lunch, but I didn't make it that easy, said maybe some other time. And other editors and their secretaries began smiling when you should smile, and saying hello. And Meehan, though he didn't go so far as to smile, spent even more time with me going over possible projects.

And this was why, when Mr. Glennie asked me to lunch for the first time, I thought it had to do only with that visit.

Mr. Glennie made it sound like an afterthought.

He had come into my cubicle to pass along copies of the *American Journal of Medicine* and *Lung*, which was unusual enough since he generally had Mrs. Dwyer do this, but then on his way out he stopped near the doorway and looked back and said, "Would you like lunch?"

"Sure."

Outside he said, "Any special place?"

"No, it doesn't matter."

He led the way to a cafeteria, and we joined the long line at the counter and stood for a while with our filled trays until he walked to a table for two set off by itself. I don't remember him saying anything for a few minutes, just concentrating on his platter of meatloaf and potatoes. I looked at him between bites of my sandwich and sips of coffee.

The first thing I remember him saying was, "When you worked at the drug company, did they have their own cafeteria?"

"Yes."

"Was it free?"

"No, but it was supposed to be cheaper than outside."

"Oh." He seemed uneasy all at once. "You could eat outside though, couldn't you?"

"Oh sure."

He nodded, but as though he were still thinking about it.
"What did you do there?"

This surprised me. He should have known from my
resumé, my interview. "I wrote booklets, papers, releases,
speeches. You know, things like that."

"Did you have anything to do with products?"

"You mean publicize them? Of course. But not everyone
handled every product. You were assigned certain ones. I did
mostly a couple of their tranquilizers, and when they lost the
patent on the big one I was out."

He returned to his platter. But he seemed to be brooding
over something as he ate. He started to say something else,
but then apparently changed his mind. And when he finally
did speak, it was about something else entirely. Nixon. And
Watergate.

"It's all politics," he said in defense of the man. "They all
do it. We don't appreciate him. Won't for years. After all, he
got us out of Vietnam. And he's opened the way with China."

I didn't feel like arguing. I'd heard all this and more from
my folks, who often wondered aloud where I came from. And
I would have heard it from at least one deceased grandfather,
who I understand had voted to reelect Hoover during the
Depression.

And now Mr. Glennie managed to kick into another topic.
"Do you know anything about pyramids?"

My face must have expressed my puzzlement, for he
immediately went on. "I have a friend who carries little pyra-
mid-shaped objects wherever he goes. He got me into
studying pyramid power." And now he was going on about

why the ancient Egyptians built their pyramids as . . . pyramids, and the energy that came from the shape itself. From that he segued into conversations he'd had with three people, living in different sections of the country, who had been abducted by aliens. Not merely claimed to have been. Had been.

Then, after about ten minutes of this, it was as though he caught himself speaking, and about what. A sheepish look came over his face.

"You've got to know," he apologized, "I'm a little crazy when it comes to this."

But it still left me wondering why he'd suddenly wanted to have lunch with me. And I never did have another one with him.

And though I am mentioning her last here, Tina Savoris had become so much on my mind that she would have been distraction enough from whatever was going on with Mr. Glennie. After I'd had that second date with her I had made up my mind that, though she was the most beautiful and sensual-looking girl I'd ever been with, had ever even seen, I didn't need being whipped back and forth anymore. And I also couldn't shake from my mind that scene of her mother berating her at their doorway, a madness I didn't want to be any part of. But only three days after that mighty resolution I was on the phone, calling her at work. Not only didn't I want to call her at home, but more important I suddenly couldn't wait until she got there. A middle-aged voice, a woman's, answered, and I asked for Miss Savoris.

"One moment."

When Tina came on, she said simply, "Yes?" and when I said, "Hi, this is Tom," it was followed by silence, and then, "Oh."

"You sound busy," I apologized, flustered. "I'm sorry. Look, I'll call you at home, if it's all right."

"No. This is all right." She was the one who sounded flustered now.

"Well, I'll make it quick. I was wondering when I might see you again."

"I really don't know. I'm busy the next few weeks. So I don't know."

"Well," not meaning it, "I'll call you again."

"I'm sorry."

And that was it. I must have said goodbye, I've always been a polite guy, but I didn't remember saying it even as I was lowering the receiver to the cradle. All I was aware of was a stupid kind of anger coursing through me, an anger at myself for doing what I'd promised I wouldn't. But this was it now. And yet two days later when I got a call from her at work, her voice almost lifted me from my chair.

"Tom, Tina. Is this a wrong time?"

"No. Not at all." I could hear the sound of automobiles through the phone, so she was calling from outside her office. It was only about two o'clock.

"I'm sorry I couldn't talk when you called," she apologized. "But I was surrounded. And this is the first chance I've had to—That's really not true," she corrected herself. "I was afraid to call, I was afraid you were angry."

"Come on."

"Look, if you can't it's all right, we'll make it some other time. But can we meet after work?"

"Sure." The words were coming out of me automatically, but they were propelled by excitement and joy. "I'll tell you what. How about the Twelfth street entrance to Manton?" This was the neighborhood park near my apartment and her office.

"That sounds good. I'll see you about a quarter after five?"

"Great."

It was only after I hung up that I began wondering what the hell I was doing, that this was just more of her whipping me back and forth. But despite my caution I kept glancing at my watch the rest of the afternoon.

One weekend every summer, Manton Park was the site of an exhibit by local artists. That Friday morning on my walk to work I had seen the artists and their helpers starting to set up, tying ropes from tree to tree from which to hang their paintings, and some of the food vendors had already been parked at the curbs. Now the park was crowded. Banners were flying. And people kept converging from office buildings and the shopping streets. I got there ten minutes before she did. I couldn't see her approaching on the sidewalk, because of the crowd, until she was almost on me. She was wearing a short skirt and clogs, the kind of shoes I didn't like, but they did nothing to distract from her great legs, distraction being the only reason I ordinarily didn't like them. She didn't hold up her cheek, let alone her lips, for a kiss. Instead she said, "I'm sorry I'm late," and squeezed my wrist.

There was something about her that soon made me think she was a little anxious. Maybe it was how, as we began walking slowly down one of the paths through the park, with paintings by different artists on either side, she barely glanced at any of them. And then suddenly she led me to a little opening to the grass and took a pack of cigarettes from her handbag and lit one with a tiny lighter. She blew out a stream of smoke, then looked at me with a strange little smile.

I said, "Are you all right?"

"It's that obvious?"

"It's that obvious."

"I'm sorry. It's just been a hell of a day."

"Do you want to go someplace else? We don't have to stay here."

"No, no. This is fine. This is what I want." She looked for some place to put out her cigarette, then ground it out against a tree and put it in a trash disposal. "I'm fine now." She took my hand and we reentered the flow on the path, then released it as she became interested in a small grouping of paintings and began talking to the young female artist sitting to one side on a beach chair.

Afterward as we walked on, she said, "I couldn't do that in a million years. I mean, the artists, sitting there watching people rejecting their work. I admire them and yet I find myself feeling sorry for them."

"They may feel sorry for us because they at least have chairs."

She looked at me puzzledly for an instant, then smiled and squeezed my hand hard before letting go.

"Hey, that really hurt," I said.

"Then no more bad jokes."

I ran into someone, a fellow I knew from the gym where I played basketball and swam a couple of times a week. We didn't talk long, but as he was leaving he gave a roll of his eyes from Tina to me. Then an elderly woman, her husband standing behind and smiling, strode to Tina and put her arms around her. It was soon apparent that she was a patient of Dr. Crestman's.

"This," the woman said to me, "is the most beautiful human being in the world. And I don't mean just her looks. She's so kind and good. And," to Tina, "how is the doctor?"

"Fine. Doing well."

"Saved my life," to me again. "And I'm just not speaking of that, but he's a great man, although"—with a little laugh— "he could use a lot of this young lady's disposition."

We circled and crisscrossed the paths of the park twice, meeting at least two other patients, each of whom embraced her and spoke as though to a longtime dear friend. I saw a number of paintings I liked, one in particular, that of an elderly man in a study, reading a book amid a pile of books.

"What do you think?" I asked her.

"It's really great."

But the price was four hundred and seventy-five dollars. Way too much for me right now.

"It's a shame," she said as we walked away. "You like it."

"I'd like a Rolls also."

"No, you don't."

"Do you mean I have to cancel my order?"

"No, I'm telling you I won't ride in it."

"Then I'll just have to cancel it and stick to my ol' Bentley." We laughed and briefly held hands as we walked.

We left the park about six-thirty to go someplace to eat. We'd both agreed on Chinese but the best restaurant in the area had a long waiting line, crowded in from the park.

"How about let's take out?" she suggested.

"Good idea."

We consulted the menus and ordered a number of things, and now we were standing on the sidewalk with the bags, and it was almost automatic when I said, "My place is right down the block," that, after looking at me for a moment, she walked along with me. But my heart suddenly was beating hard.

We put the bags on the card table that was my dining room table and I opened up two bridge chairs. I pulled back the folding doors that opened to the kitchen unit along the wall, and got out plates and utensils.

I said, "If you use chop sticks, I'm sorry. I should have asked for some."

"Don't be sorry. I even use a knife."

"What do you think I have here?" I held up knives I was bringing to the table.

"Wonderful."

"Of course, when I use them with Chinese I always pull down the shades."

She laughed as she set the table. Then, when we were sitting, she said, "You've got a nice little place here." And it was. A sofa-bed, closed, was along one wall, with a cocktail table in front of it. There were a couple of comfortable chairs, and a hard one in front of my electric typewriter, and a large AM/FM radio—I hadn't replaced a worn-out TV—on one of the windowsills next to the window with the air conditioner. A few shelves of books hung near the chairs, and the walls held a number of prints. A hall led to the bathroom and closets.

She said, her voice almost anguished, "I wish I could find a place like this."

"Can't you?"

"Well, I could . . . But I'm going to be leaving my job."

"Really? When did you decide this?"

"Oh, I've been thinking about it for a while."

I didn't press on with this line of conversation—it seemed too upsetting to her—until we were almost finished eating. I said, "That woman in the park who said she wished Dr. Crestman had your disposition. I don't mean to get personal, but is he a tough guy?"

"Not really," she said quickly. "I mean . . . well, sometimes. But he's brilliant, he really is, he's a brilliant man," as though that would compensate for anything.

"You know," I said, "I first heard of him when I was with Packer-Hill. But I never met him."

But it was as though she didn't hear. She went on with: "My leaving has nothing to do with him. It's just time I did. I think I would like to go back being a nurse."

"You can't with him?"

"No."

We were down to our fortune cookies. I was to find happiness living in the country. She was simply good at numbers.

"My God," she said, "I can barely add."

She laughed, but the smile afterward didn't last. Looking at her, I thought of a line I'd read somewhere, I couldn't think where, but it came under "words of advice": never get involved with a woman who has more troubles than you do.

She said, aloud but really to herself, "And I've got to get out of that house."

"Can't you? I mean, can you find a place and hold onto the job until you get another one?"

"I guess. I guess."

She frowned, then stood up and began gathering the dishes to take to the sink. We both cleared the table, and I went out to the hallway to throw the garbage down the chute. When I came back she was looking at the books on the wall.

"Did you edit any of these?"

"No."

She kept looking at them, and when she turned she was looking squarely at me. I put my arms around her and brought her to me. There was no resistance this time, not the slightest. Our mouths met, opened; she twisted her face against mine, her palms on the back of my head. I began touching her, her covered breasts, her back, and then began unbuttoning her blouse while she was almost tearing at my shirt. But now that we were naked and on the unopened sofa, I was aware then, and even before, that this wasn't working for me. I was trying to think passion, to force it into me and through me, but I felt none of it; only the want. I wanted. Yet I couldn't shake away my uneasiness with this girl, or slow the quick, nervous beating of my heart.

I rose slowly and she came up with me. I kept holding her in my arms. This time her head sank against my shoulder.

I thought of the pack of weed under the bathroom sink. But I didn't go for it. For some reason, even if it helped, I didn't want this that way.

"Where did you get that?" she asked. She was pointing to a print of Emmet Kelley, the sad-faced clown. It was as though nothing unusual had happened.

"In New York. Greenwich Village. Actually it's the first picture I ever bought."

"I like it. I like it very much. And I see you don't have a TV."

"Oh, I had one but it died," I joked weakly.

"Now that sounds very sad."

"Actually it isn't. I found I can live without it."

I could feel my heart gradually slowing.

I said, "Can I ask you a silly question?"

"That's the kind I like."

"Did you ever work in your father's pizza parlor?"

"No. And anyway it isn't his."

"You said it was."

"I know. I lied."

"Oh? And did you kill all those people?"

"Which people?"

"I don't know. Since you're not lying now I thought I'd ask you a good question."

"It was a terrible question."

"Tell me. Why did you lie about your father?"

She shrugged her naked shoulders. "I guess I just wanted him to be boss."

I looked at her. That struck me as so sad. Her eyes were almost closed. We were in a terribly awkward position on that sofa. One of my legs was off it. I wriggled it back up and she opened her eyes briefly and then closed them again.

I couldn't get over how she didn't make fun, ridicule, question, blame herself, blame anything, ask what was wrong.

I stroked her hair, her forehead. She opened her eyes, and closed them when I kissed her eyelids. She whispered, "You don't have to do—" but I put my forefinger on her lips. I kissed her mouth, softly, and soon her lips stirred and they were soft in their response too. She was touching at my hair. I could feel her head crane to watch as I kissed each breast.

And now as we made love, with her breath quick in my ear, and then quicker still, I could feel her body tighten and rise, then rise some more, and, after several moments, so very gradually ease down with me. We lay tumbled together, half on the floor.

When, some time afterward, I touched her cheek, I was surprised to feel the cool wetness of tears.

I thought only that it was out of happiness. And maybe it was.

Chapter Ten

It's strange, no weird, how I always associate the following Tuesday with sunshine. It was such a foreboding day—certainly in retrospect—and yet my memory of it always takes in the sight of sunshine through the windows as I walked from the elevator to my cubicle. The next image, though it was sometime later, is that of Mrs. Dwyer standing in my doorway. She looked concerned.

"Have you heard from Mr. Glennie?"

"No." And it was only then that I glanced at my wristwatch. It was twenty of ten.

She frowned, then walked away. About an hour later, after a quick look in his office, I walked over to her desk.

"Have you heard from him?"

"No. And I don't understand it."

When he still hadn't showed up by one, I approached her again. "This is very unusual for him, isn't it?"

"Very. In fact I don't remember the last time he took off, let alone was late, without at least calling."

"Do you think we should call his home?"

She looked at me as if I'd said something dreadful. "No, I don't want to do that. I mean, you can but I'd rather not. I don't want him to think I'm prying."

Sometime later on Meehan, in his usual brown suit and holding some papers, stepped into my cubicle just long enough to look around, as though I might be hiding Mr. Glennie. Then he left without a word. Soon afterward Troy

66

Roper started to pass by, then stopped and tilted his head toward me. "I hear he hasn't showed up today."

"Seems that way." I wanted to keep it light with him.

He grinned and stepped in a little way. "Maybe he took off in that spaceship of his."

"Troy"—I still hated his guts but had begun calling him Troy—"what're you talking about?" But I was thinking of that remark about a spaceship Mr. Glennie himself had made to me.

"Oh?" He came in closer, and suddenly I regretted asking: it made me feel like a kind of conspirator in Mr. Glennie's absence. His grin widened. "He got looped once and told someone he'd invested in a real honest to God spaceship. Bought stock in it."

"Well," I tried to defend him, "I think we can put that one away, don't you?"

"I heard he was serious. I don't know who was building it, maybe some handyman for all I know." He gave a little laugh, and before leaving repeated it: "A handyman. I wouldn't be surprised."

I just sat there, staring after him. The truth was, though it was absolutely crazy, I wouldn't have been all that surprised either.

It was about four-thirty when I put aside the copyediting I was doing and sat there at my desk very much aware that I didn't even know where Mr Glennie lived. I walked out to Mrs. Dwyer.

"You still haven't heard anything, have you?"

"No." She looked at me with a wince.

"Could I have his phone number? I don't have it."

She immediately reached for her listings, obviously relieved I was going to do what she felt she didn't have the right to do. Back at my desk I dialed the number, then again.

It kept ringing on and on.

Tina called that evening, exuberant. "Well, I did it."

"Whatever it is, congratulations."

"I got an apartment."

"Oh? Terrific. Wonderful."

"And I'm in it. Not at this very second. I don't have a phone yet and I'm calling from a pay phone."

"Well, this really calls for congratulations."

She explained that she'd seen an ad in this morning's paper about a furnished apartment a few blocks from her office that seemed just right, and she'd left work to see it, had taken it, then had gone home by cab and brought back enough of her things for a few days.

"Wow. How did your folks take it?"

"Oh . . . Like they finally had it. My father hadn't gone to work yet, and he just raised his hands, like 'If that's what you want.' And my mother, she muttered a lot but she more or less just went along."

"Can I help you get the rest of your stuff?"

"I appreciate that, but no. It's better I do it my way."

"Well, congratulations again."

"I've got a very nice kitchen. The whole place is nice, but there is this kitchen. I'll make you moussaka. I make a delicious moussaka, if I say so myself."

"That's like a BLT, isn't it?"

"Yes, exactly." Then she laughed.

I asked if we could get together that evening, but she said, apologetically, that she wanted to get started on fixing up the apartment, there was a lot she had to do, but could we tomorrow?

"Of course."

It was only about fifteen minutes after I hung up that

the phone rang again.

"Is this Mr. Loberg?" a woman asked.

"Yes."

"I'm sorry to call you at this hour, but I hope you don't mind. This is Mrs. Glennie. Samuel's wife."

"Oh, don't be sorry, please." My hand had tightened on the phone.

"I've been away with the children since yesterday and we just got home and Samuel's not here. Was he at the office today?"

I hated to say it. "No, he wasn't."

"Oh . . ." It held a soft sound of anguish. "Was he there yesterday?"

"Yes."

"Oh God. He never came home. Our bed wasn't slept in."

I wasn't sure what to say. "When did you see him last?"

"When he left for work yesterday. He seemed all right. Everything seemed all right."

"Have you"—again, I hated to say it—"called any hospitals?"

"No." Her voice was faint.

"How about his friends? Have you called any of his friends?"

"A couple. They don't . . ."

"What about anyone else at work? How about Mr. Meehan?"

"No." Still faint. Then a sob broke through. "I-I'm sorry. I'm sorry. But I hate them, I hate them all!"

Chapter Eleven

As I approached the building the next morning, I could feel the twisting of tension as I wondered whether or not I'd find him there. It wasn't quite nine when I got off the elevator, and usually he was in long before that. But as I approached our section Mrs. Dwyer, hanging up her coat, looked at me in a way that said he wasn't in yet.

I gave it ten more minutes, then went to my doorway. She looked up from her typing and, her face grave, gave a little shake of her head. I gestured for her to come in.

"Mrs. Glennie called me last night. She wanted to know if I'd heard from him."

"Oh God." A hand lifted to her mouth.

"Tell me, when he left here Monday, did he seem sick or depressed?"

"No. Not that I could tell."

"Do you know if this has happened before? I mean where he doesn't show up at home?"

"I wouldn't know that, but I doubt that very much."

"You know," I said, "I don't even know where he lives."

"He lives in Crayton." One of the sections of the city, near the outskirts.

"Does he drive? Do you know if he drives to work?"

"I know he's been taking the train lately. Ever since the gas shortage. But I don't know if he did it Monday."

I debated whether to tell Meehan about Mrs. Glennie's call. But I kept thinking of her I hate them, I hate them all, and it was as though I would be betraying her. But about fifteen minutes later Meehan came to me. His little face was tight, but it was more out of annoyance and distaste than anger.

"So he's not in, he's still not in."

I thought: you bastard, I'll give you something to worry about. "I spoke to his wife last night. She called me. He never came home Monday and she hasn't heard from him. Wanted to know if I heard from him."

But if it worried him he didn't show it. He just frowned. And then with that same look of annoyance, he walked out shaking his head.

Troy Roper came in a little later. "I hear still nothing."

"You got it."

He walked closer to my desk. Then, after a glance over his shoulder, "He's a closet alkie. I'll bet anything on that."

I just looked at him.

"I know the type," he said. Then, with a little smile, "I know one other thing—he didn't run away with a lady."

I still said nothing.

"Can you see him running off with a lady?" he pressed. And then when he saw I still didn't think that was funny, he said, "He'll be back," and left with a little wave.

I tried to work but couldn't. My thoughts kept going back to Monday, to what he'd looked like, how he'd acted. But, of the little I'd seen of him, nothing stood out. I did remember seeing him leave, though, a hulking figure holding a beat-up-looking satchel, probably of work he'd continue with at home. He hadn't said good night. Nor, a fast learner, had I. We'd just nodded at each other.

Meehan and Roper were probably right: he'd simply show up; if anything serious had happened to him we'd surely have heard about it by now. And it wasn't as if I loved the guy.

Even liked him. I hated him most of the time, not real hate, understand, a kind of hate, and not because of anything he did to me but because of what he'd let them do to him. And even now, with his disappearance, you'd think the bastards would at least show a little concern! After all these years, a little concern!

But Meehan never even came to me again that day, nor, as I learned from her, to Mrs. Dwyer. The most that happened was that, on one or two occasions, I noticed other of the editors looking over our way, as if they would see something to satisfy their curiosity.

About four o'clock, after a lot of thought, I called the Glennie home. And was instantly sorry. Mrs. Glennie picked up the phone so fast that I knew it was with the hope it was her husband.

"It's just me, Mrs. Glennie. Tom Loberg. I'm sorry to bother you."

"No, no, no." Then she began to cry. "I-I'm sorry."

"God, don't be."

"I'm sorry." I could hear her taking deep breaths. "But I still haven't heard anything. I-I've called the police . . . I don't know."

"I'll hang up," I said. "I know you want to leave the phone open."

"Yes." She said it almost absently.

"If I can do anything for you, please feel free to call me."

"Yes. I appreciate that, Thomas."

My heart was drumming as I hung up. I just sat there, staring at the phone. I still felt as if I'd done a dumb thing calling. But I'd had to know, and now it was hard holding on to any kind of hope. I just couldn't see him leaving his ox-like day-to-day ways to suddenly take off. I could see him murdered for a few dollars and his body waiting to be found. I could see him, say, cracking up maybe; but his wife would have heard from some hospital by now, wouldn't she?

I had called Tina earlier and I was to meet her right after work to see her apartment. The air was hazy in the sun and just a perfect-touch cool as I walked away from the flow out of the Mallory & Mallory building. We arrived at the same time at the front steps of her building, a row house that had been converted to three apartments. Hers was on the second floor, rear, away from the noises of the street and overlooking a little garden.

Taking me by the hand, she led me through it, a compressed one-bedroom, with in fact a kitchen that was larger than the other rooms. The furniture, she said with a laugh, was "early seashore rooming-house," but she didn't mind at all. We kissed in the living room, a long kiss, and afterward held each other and then kissed again.

I looked at her and touched at the hair over her forehead. She smiled and kissed me quickly on the lips.

"I promised you moussaka, but not tonight."

"Really? Oh, I'm leaving."

"I ran out and had just enough time to buy a few basics. And I was lucky to even remember to buy a frying pan."

"Well, we're eating out anyway, to celebrate."

"I can make us omelets."

"No, we'll go out and—"

"I make good omelets."

"How good?"

"Real good."

"Do you use eggs?"

She looked at me, head tilted. "No. Pebbles."

"You mean we'll get stoned?"

"Look, I don't like bad jokes." But she was smiling. "Let's

eat here, if it's okay. I'm anxious to use my kitchen."

So, my first meal there was an omelet, which was indeed good. And I was surprised to learn that she liked classical music, almost all of it, which was further than I went. She'd brought a small radio from home, and it was tuned in to a classical music station as we ate.

Samuel Wallace Glennie had slipped almost from my thoughts. But whenever he did rise up, it was with a quick burning in my chest.

I looked at her next to me on the bed, her bare shoulders showing just above the sheet. Her eyes were closed. She wore, I had noticed for the first time that evening, no makeup. But there was a touch of pink, perhaps still from our lovemaking, on the one cheek I could see.

She opened her eyes, as though sensing I was looking at her. She smiled.

"Have I been asleep long?"

"Just from yesterday."

Her eyes went closed, then after a few moments opened again. "Hold me."

I held her, and she held onto me. "Now go. I don't want you to, but go."

"Then why is youse suddenly kickin' me out?"

"I ain't kickin' you out. Well, maybe. There's an old, old couple on the floor and I have the feeling they're waiting to see how long it takes before I bring in sailors. I'd like to first live here at least a week."

"Good rule."

I got dressed, then walked with her to the door. I put my arms around her and we kissed good night. The radio was still playing. I was barely aware that the news was on. Until I heard, ". . . found early this evening in the Pawtoni River."

74

I drew back slowly from her.

"Tom, what's wrong?"

I didn't answer right away. Had I heard—I thought I'd heard—that the body had been identified as—who?—something-or-other Glennie?

Chapter Twelve

The first thing I did when I got back to my apartment was huddle over the radio and begin searching for news. But it wasn't until about two o'clock, in bed but still unable to fall asleep, that I heard it. And the next day's paper that I picked up at the drugstore gave fuller details. A fully clothed body, identified as Samuel Wallace Glennie, 57, had been found Wednesday evening floating near the east bank of the Pawtoni River. He had been missing since late Monday afternoon, when he left work, ostensibly to walk to the train station. His wallet, which appeared untouched, had been found on him; and according to preliminary reports, the body showed no signs of wounds or bruises.

"Mr. Glennie, manager of Special Projects at Mallory and Mallory Publishers," the story continued, "was married and the father of three children . . ."

Three? That just about leaped up at me. Mrs. Dwyer had definitely told me two.

Even in death, I thought, he's getting screwed.

As I walked on to work I felt anxious. Sad but mostly anxious. I didn't doubt for an instant—there was no reason to doubt it—that he had committed suicide, that he'd finally crumbled after years of being beat up on. And though days had gone by when we barely talked to each other, I felt adrift and a growing loneliness about that place I was heading to.

I don't know what I expected when I got there; anyway, something different, something totally different from the usual. But the only thing I saw in those few minutes before nine was something I often saw, a group of the secretaries, Mrs. Dwyer among them, standing by one of their desks, a few sipping coffee. Then Mrs. Dwyer came back. The look on her face was one of bewilderment. She glanced at me, then away, as though that would make her cry and she mustn't here. She was touching some paper clips on her desk when I said, "Mrs. Dwyer, whenever you can," at which she slowly followed me back to my cubicle.

I said, suddenly not knowing what else to say, "This is terrible."

She nodded quickly, teeth on her lower lip. And all I could still think of was clichés.

"I didn't have any idea," I said. "What was he like when he left here? I didn't talk to him."

"Himself. Just himself."

"He had two children, didn't he? The paper said three."

"No, he had two."

I could see Meehan heading this way down the aisle, that one shoulder of his forward. This, I thought, should be beautiful.

"Police!" He'd barely entered my cubicle. He was almost sputtering. "Call me at my home! Middle of the night! 'What was he like?' Middle of the night! The damn fool!"

And then like a thin whirlwind in a brown suit he was gone.

I looked at Mrs. Dwyer. But she didn't seem at all dismayed by him.

"He did do a terrible thing," she said solemnly, with a shake of her head. "Terrible. And that poor family of his."

Troy Roper came by, but only to shake his head and say, "He really did it, didn't he?" and to linger just long enough to realize he wasn't getting a reply from me. A couple of other editors stopped by at different times, to find out, not too subtly, if there was anything scandalously new. Then Mrs. Dwyer came in again, this time to lay some letters on my desk. All of them were addressed to Mr. Glennie.

"I thought I should give them to you."

When she left, I picked them up and opened them—they were things like bills from the printer, ads for paper stock—then I put them back in their envelopes and dealt them onto my desk, one by one.

I recalled her saying she had been with the company twenty-two years, working for someone else, then moved over to Mr. Glennie when he came here fourteen years ago.

Now it was my turn.

The Pawtoni, a wide, quiet river free of commercial ships that cut across the length of the city, was about two miles from the station where Mr. Glennie would have taken the train. I wondered if he'd made up his mind here in the office and walked straight to the river, holding onto that beatup leather satchel of his. Or had he gone first to the station, and there snapped his mind shut of any other decision, and come back out to walk on again? I tried to picture, not for any purpose but just thinking of him, which street he might have taken on that walk. One of those with little restaurants and antique shops, opening suddenly to the sparkling—on these days, certainly—river?

I wondered—again for no real reason—about his satchel. Had he dropped it in a trash can along the way, or tossed it in the river before leaping from one of the two high, suspension bridges that spanned it, or maybe even carried it with him as he walked down any of the sloping banks and out into the water to depth? I wondered if there'd been any fishermen out —there usually were at certain places—and whether any sculls or other small boats had been anywhere around. And why would he have done it in daylight, if he had done it in daylight, or had he brooded about it for hours, perhaps in some bar, until dark?

I found myself thinking of another suicide that had had an impact on me. It had happened way back when I was nine. A next door neighbor, an elderly man named Cummings, was so bereaved by the sudden death of his wife that he even used to stop us kids on the sidewalk and, crying, tell us how much he missed her. Then one morning I woke up to learn that he had gone into his basement while I'd been sleeping and put a bullet through the roof of his mouth. I was thinking of it now partly, I guess, because the two deaths were so different. With Mr. Cummings, though a shock, it had been no surprise. With Mr. Glennie, no one who saw him Monday could have guessed that that day would be different from any other.

And so a part of me started to cling, though ever so slightly, to the possibility that instead of suicide he'd been killed or somehow had fallen accidentally into the river. But then I remembered something else. One of the things I'd written about at Packer-Hill, concerning its antidepressants, was that not every suicidal person looks or acts depressed. Quite the contrary. Some seem quite content, having reached the decision that they are going to kill themselves.

But a phone call I got later that day had me confused again.

It came a little after three-thirty.

"Mr. Loberg."

Somehow I instantly recognized Mrs. Glennie's voice even though it was low, faint.

"Yes," I said, leaning forward with the phone, "this is Tom, Mrs. Glennie."

"Please do me a favor. Will you do me a big favor?"

"Of course. Just tell me."

"I—I hate to trouble you, Thomas, I hate to make you go through this, but would you go in Samuel's office and save something for me?"

"Of course."

"I'll have someone come down and clean out all his things, but I don't know when that will be, and I don't want to lose this. And it's so small. It's a watch. I don't know whether it's on his desk or in one of his drawers, but would you look for it for me?"

"I'll go look now. I'll call you right back."

As I passed Mrs. Dwyer's desk I said, "Mrs. Glennie just called. She wants me to look for something in his desk and save it."

Her face showed just a bit of wonder, or maybe crossness that Mrs. Glennie had called me and not her. I was puzzled myself.

It was a little eerie being in the quiet of that office. I moved aside papers and various things on the top of the desk but couldn't come up with it. But I did find it in the first drawer I opened, the top one on the right. There was nothing fancy about the watch; it was simply a plain wristwatch, one of the cheaper brands.

Back at my desk I called Mrs. Glennie. I was looking at the watch as I dialed. Then it hit me all at once that it was set at twenty after one. Curious, I tried to set the hands to the right time—but they wouldn't move.

"Hello?" It was a girl's voice.

"May I speak to your mother? Mrs. Glennie?"

She came on. "Yes."

"This is Tom, Mrs. Glennie. I just want you to know that I have it."

"Thank you." Then there was silence, then out of it came sobbing. "I-I'm sorry, I'm really sorry. I hate to do this to you, I hate to burden you. But Samuel didn't kill himself! I know it, I know it! He couldn't have, he wouldn't have!"

Chapter Thirteen

Just that and no more. It was as though those words had flung themselves from her, after which she said in a trembling voice, "I'm sorry to do this to you, I really am," and then quietly hung up. I sat there for several dazed moments before realizing she was gone. I picked up the phone quickly to call her back, but this died in the realization that I had nothing to say. Absolutely nothing.

My immediate feeling was a terrible sadness that she was clinging to the belief that he hadn't deliberately abandoned her and their children. But who would have murdered that quiet, selfless man? Sure, it could have been something mindless, a robbery that went wrong. But what about the money still in his wallet? And no bruises on him? And what had he been doing by the river anyway? Why would he have walked on from the train station, except to kill himself?

Still, what out of all their years of closeness did his wife know of him with a certainty that none of us could begin to know?

And then I thought of something that, in its own way, made killing weirdly logical here. It would be a fitting finality to his life, wouldn't it, if the poor guy was actually murdered and it went undetected?

I walked out of that building into sunshine. It had rained that morning and through much of the day, so that now the late afternoon seemed doubly bright. It was one of the few days that I'd driven to work, and as I walked to the parking lot I felt a kind of reluctance to go right home, to enter what felt like the darkness of an apartment. But as I started to pull out of the lot, I understood what was holding me back. I was being drawn to the river.

I took the street that was the most direct route from Mallory & Mallory. As I drove, with restaurants and shops on either side, I thought of him walking here; and at the corner where he would have turned to go to the train station, I wondered again if he'd made that turn, only to change his mind. I drove on, and the street opened to the river, glittery in the still-strong sun. Two one-man sculls were skimming by, not racing but keeping pace with each other.

Many shops, bars and restaurants ran parallel to the river, on Devon Street. To my left was the high, arching 23rd Street Bridge, and several miles to my right, out of sight from here, was the even longer Cornell. If Mr. Glennie had come onto the river at this point to jump from the walkway of a bridge, it would have been the 23rd Street. If he'd simply crossed over Devon Street around here to leap from the embankment, he'd had a fairly high wall to climb—and perhaps dozens of eyes to watch. Unless, that is, he'd waited—but where?—until dark.

But would I have waited?

I was barely aware, at first, how I was putting myself in his place.

If I waited, I would have to start thinking more about my wife, about the girls. Could I kill myself after this long pondering? I had a hard time thinking yes.

I drove left on Devon and soon came to clusters of warehouses, where the river wasn't even in view from the street. Here I would have to climb fences and go through gates to reach it. I began driving to the right now, and in this direction, as I knew, I came to Glowden Park after a couple of miles. Here the banks to the river were low, with a little incline. Several fishermen were standing about, a couple of them in boots in the edges of the water.

I pulled into a gravel lane and parked facing the river. A motorboat passed, its motor almost turned off; two women in a canoe were approaching in slow, deliberate rhythm. Anywhere around here would be the easiest place to slip in. But this would also have meant at least a two-mile longer walk.

Could he—his body?—have been driven here for dumping?

But Christ, Glennie? *Glennie?* There were plenty of reasons to think him a fool, whatever. But who in God's name could have possibly hated that gentle man so much?

It was almost uncanny, as though the police had been watching me playing detective. But it was only a few minutes after I got back to the apartment when I got a call from a detective.

"This is Detective Orster, from the Third Division. Am I speaking to"—he paused, as though reading from something—"Mr. Loberg? Thomas Loberg?"

"That's right."

"I'm looking into the death of Mr. Samuel Glennie. I understand you worked with him."

"Yes. Actually he was my boss."

"Right." He drawled the word, as if still reading. "Tom" —I was suddenly Tom to him—"I wonder if we could get together for a few minutes. Like now, in fact. Would you happen to be free? Actually I'm in the neighborhood."

"Now would be fine."

He read off my address to me, just to make sure of it, and less than fifteen minutes later he was buzzing the intercom.

He was a man of about fifty, hefty, wearing a light wind-breaker with a badge dangling from one of the pockets, and a checkered cap.

"Naah," he said, when I offered that he sit down. Then, taking out a little notebook, "I've talked to a couple people and I don't see where this should take long. Now, you knew the deceased how long?"

"About five months."

"Did he ever talk suicide to you?"

"No. There was no hint of it."

"Was he acting differently in any way?"

I started to say no, but then checked myself. "One thing, he started smoking recently. Smoking again, that is, though I'd never seen him smoke before."

"Smoke?"

"You asked if there was anything different. And that's the only thing I can think of. Oh, and this is nothing at all, but about a week ago he invited me out to lunch for the first time."

"Any special reason?"

"No. I can't think of any. He wanted to know about the kind of work I'd been doing before. And he talked quite a bit about UFOs, if that's of any interest. He liked to visit places where they've been sighted."

"Yeah, I heard." But he seemed to be thinking of something else. Then he said, "Do you know of any enemies he might have had?"

"No, not really."

"What does not really mean?"

"Well, often he was like the butt of jokes at work. But that didn't seem to bother him."

"I heard that too." He looked at his notebook, though he'd barely written anything in it. Then he closed it and looked at me. "So you're one of the editors," he said.

"Yes."

"Do you . . ." He hesitated. "Do you handle mysteries?"

And all at once I knew why he'd wanted to stop over rather than ask those few questions on the phone. Instead of answering, I said, "Do you write them?"

"Not yet, but I'm thinking of it. I've got lots of ideas and I've been making notes."

"Well, I myself don't handle them but when you're ready I can point you to someone who does."

"Yeah?"

"I certainly can."

He smiled. "I'll remember that. The other people I spoke to, they said they only do doctors."

"Well, I can refer you to someone."

"I'll bear that in mind." He smiled and stuck out his hand. "Good talking to you."

"Good talking to you."

He reached for the doorknob, then stopped and said, "There's no doubt he did himself. No doubt."

I looked at him. "I'm sure you know," I said, "it's not what his wife believes."

"I know." He nodded slightly. "It's a hard thing to take." He looked at me a moment longer. "Take it easy."

I watched as he walked off down the hall.

Chapter Fourteen

I returned Mr. Glennie's watch to his widow a few days later at the small, neighborhood funeral parlor, the Belheim Brothers Mortuary, where the services were held. A little more than thirty people were there, sitting on folding chairs. The dull brown casket lay closed behind a lectern; both were up on a kind of stage. There were three large bouquets of flowers in front of the coffin. He was to be cremated.

As I looked at the casket from one of the back rows I kept picturing him in there, all bloated, his shoulders squeezed in. I was back to thinking him a suicide—it was such an easy, uncomplicated slide—and couldn't help thinking, sadly but with anger I had no right to feel: you poor sad boob.

I'd gone up to Mrs. Glennie before the service, a fairly heavyset, plain-looking woman in a black dress, and told her who I was, and as I gave her the watch she took my hand with great strength and emotion and thanked me softly for it, and then even for coming. Her daughters, one about fifteen, the other a couple of years younger, sat on each side of her. They were both dark-haired and in black dresses and, though more attractive, looked remarkably like their mother.

I was surprised, though I shouldn't have been, that the only ones there from the office were Meehan, Mrs. Dwyer and her husband, and an editor by the name of Bertram Hams, whom I'd never as much as seen talking with Mr. Glennie. I was sharply aware that the president, Wilfred

Mallory III, wasn't there, nor was anyone else from the down-stairs' executive offices.

A priest walked to the lectern. I would hear later that both Glennies, products of Catholic schools, had given up on organized religion but that she had come to know this priest through some volunteer hospice work she'd done. But what followed was hardly much of a religious service, let alone a Mass. It quickly became apparent that he hadn't even known Mr. Glennie, for there was nothing personal about the little sermon he gave, which consisted of little more than clichés such as, believe it or not, "he was a good father and hus-band." Nothing about suicide, and nothing about possible murder; it was as though it were natural to be found dead in a river. He read a passage from John, I believe, and afterward asked for Jesus' blessings on "the deceased, Samuel Wallace Glennie, and his family." And he seemed glad to give up the lectern to Mr. Glennie's two daughters, though only one of them spoke. "He was a great daddy," and while the younger one cried, the older one, before breaking down, told of such things as how he used to take them fishing for trout, and how he would motivate them to do their best in everything, including reading good books. And the next speaker was a woman who spoke of how "Samuel" rejuvenated a book club some of them in the neighborhood had started, had gotten them reading writers such as Melville and Balzac.

Afterward, when we were all standing up and starting to drift off, a man I'd barely noticed during the service came up to me. He introduced himself as Mrs. Glennie's nephew.

"Edith told me to ask you to join us at the house for lunch, if it's at all possible."

"Yes. Of course."

But I wondered why someone hadn't announced from the lectern that everyone was invited to the house. Then the obvious struck me, that they weren't asking everyone. But then why me?

The Glennie house was one in a curved line of twin houses that formed an isolated cul-de-sac near the outskirts of the city. About twenty people were there, standing about, some already eating the food and drinking the drinks that were on the dining room table. They had beer among the hard liquor and sodas, and I took one, more to hold something in my hand than anything else.

Now and then I would look over at Mrs. Glennie, who was standing in the living room talking to people as they came up. Her daughters were with a couple of other young girls, and the thing that hit me instantly was that they were smiling. Again I thought: you poor goddamn boob!

"Wonderful man, wasn't he?"

He'd come up to me, holding a drink, a short man who identified himself as a neighbor.

"Yes he was."

"May I ask how you know him?"

"I worked with him. He was my boss."

His lips formed an o. "Then you know what a brilliant man he was. Knew about everything. One of those who did the *New York Times* puzzle with a pen. And did you know he was quite a bowler?"

"No, I didn't."

"We used to have a bowling league here. This was before a lot of the old neighbors moved out. There's hardly anyone today you know well enough to speak to anymore. But he was quite a bowler, though we haven't done it in years. In fact we used to have some great parties down in the basement. Great parties."

I wanted to say: really? It was taking a lot of adjustment to think of Mr. Glennie bowling or even giving a party, let alone a great one.

"It had to be an accident," the neighbor went on, his voice lowering and suddenly solemn, "or . . . or something." It was as if he couldn't say the word murder. "No way what they're all saying. He would never do that. No way." He looked at me intently, then nodded and sauntered away.

An accident? I hadn't given that even an instant's thought, and dismissed it immediately. To walk to a train station on your way home, and then go two more miles to—what?—look at a river?—and then accidentally fall in? Sorry, no.

But murder was again at the front of my mind.

Uneasy, I began drifting around. I looked at the food-covered table in the dining room but couldn't think of eating. Then I wandered over to the books that lined and overflowed the walls on either side of the entrance to the dining room. They were in no particular order—classics intermingled with popular and not-so-popular novels and non-fiction. I noticed that there were no sets, no identically-bound "Complete Works of . . ." Mr. Glennie hadn't bought for "show," only individual books he liked or was curious about. But then I noticed something that seemed mighty strange. On one of the shelves were four novels, held together and separated from the other books by bronze bookends. They were Thomas Wolfe's *Look Homeward Angel*, Hemingway's *The Sun Also Rises*, Scott Fitzgerald's *The Great Gatsby*, and Marjorie Kinnan Rawlings' *The Yearling*. I wondered why those four books in particular? Then after quite a struggle, something came to me, the only unifying thing I could think of: that their authors shared the same editor, the legendary Max Perkins.

Had Mr. Glennie, bent over his vanity manuscripts and proofs, ever dreamed of some day being a Max Perkins? And when had that dream died?

"This is Samuel's," Mrs. Glennie's voice suddenly spoke behind me.

For an instant I didn't know what she meant.

"This one, this is Samuel's," and she reached over and took down a book and handed it to me. It was a novel called *The Poe Prescription*, and under the title were the words A Mystery, and under that in fairly large print Samuel Wallace Glennie. Astonished, I turned it over and saw on the spine that it was published by Alfred Knopf, and there on the back was a young Mr. Glennie smiling. I started to look to see when it was published, and she said, "That was 1948. He was thirty-two."

I looked at her, feeling stupid. "He never mentioned this to me."

"Oh, I'm not surprised. That was Samuel."

"Did he write any others?"

"He wrote a second one but they didn't take it, and a couple other publishers didn't take it, and he just gave up. I tried to tell him, 'Look, all it means is that these few places don't want it, or it just doesn't fit in with their plans, but they're not all the publishers in the world, and you've also got other things you can write . . .' But there was no talking to him. And we did need money, we had one of the children by then . . . He was such a marvelous father," she said, her eyelids closed for a moment. "Almost every minute he wasn't working he was doing things with them, with us."

I opened the book, to no particular page but just to look at something I hadn't dreamed he'd done. Then her voice said:

"He liked you, Tom."

I looked up at her quickly. Her eyes were glazed. It had been so startling to hear—and even that I was no longer "Thomas" to her—that it chilled me.

"We used to talk about it," she continued, with a little smile now while wiping at her eyes. "He—he was terribly insecure," as if I didn't know. "He worried about his job all the time, and you—I hope you'll forgive me—you were a threat, particularly at the beginning. We used to talk about it a lot, and I used to say, 'Samuel, a threat to what? Who wants that lousy job of yours?' And we'd laugh. And he came to like you very much. I know that. That's why I wanted you here. I wouldn't have otherwise. You'll notice—no one else from that place."

"Yes, I have noticed."

"He was such a good, good soul. He never held a grudge, a hate against anyone. He even"—she smiled—"had great compassion for Nixon. We had so many arguments about that." Then, serious again, "And even Mrs. Dwyer. Be careful of her. Don't tell her anything you don't want everyone else to hear. It happened a couple of times with Samuel but I couldn't even get him to change secretaries. He was afraid it would get her fired."

It was becoming hard for all this to sink in. "Mrs. Glennie, may I ask you something? That wristwatch in his office—may I ask why it's so special?"

She looked at me. "Well, you'll think Samuel was crazy. But he was given that by a man, an elderly man in Oklahoma —" She hesitated. "A man who said he was visited by someone from outer space. And when the alien left, the man's watch, which had been working perfectly, was frozen. And Samuel bought it from him. I'd be embarrassed to tell you how much he paid for it. And so it is special to me. It holds a certain memory."

Her eyes stayed on me. "I guess," she said with a faint smile, "you've been there long enough to have heard about a . . . spaceship?"

"Yes," I said uncertainly.

"But they don't know why. I'll bet anything they don't know why. Oh, Samuel, Samuel," she said with a sigh. "Yes, we invested in that crazy idea. He pleaded with me to let him do it. It was a legitimate company, I understand, but of course a terrible, terrible idea. And, no surprise, they went under."

I was about to ask her something when a woman approached her. Mrs Glennie, turning to me before walking off with her, said, "Will you be here a while? I want to explain that."

"Yes, I'll be here."

But when she did come back, about an hour later, she was embarrassed that she'd told me to wait.

"I'm sorry," she apologized. "You've got other things—"

"No. Please. I'm honored that you told me."

She looked at me. She appeared to be trying to make up her mind about something. Then, "Let's, would you mind, let's go out front." But there, on the small lawn near the steps, she lowered her head and didn't seem to know how to begin. When she looked up, it was almost defiantly. "I don't care who you tell this to. I just don't want them at that place to think he was crazy. I mean crazy in a bad way. If he was crazy he was crazy in a good way."

I almost had to force myself to stand there and look at her. I didn't want to know any secrets of a family I knew nothing about. And yet, perversely, I wanted to know.

"She was terribly malformed," Mrs. Glennie was saying, as though to herself.

I just waited. Growing more uneasy, tense.

"She was our first, is our first. Our little Janie. But so terribly, terribly malformed and—and retarded. She's been in a place, an institution, ever since, ever since she was born. You can't begin to imagine. And Samuel didn't want us to talk about her. Oh, we have, to some people, to family. But Samuel had this vision of her coming out some day and being perfectly normal, and everyone really seeing her for the first time. That's how he wanted them to see her and think of her. And that's—that's when he first got interested in outer space, in UFOs."

She was looking at me, as if studying me for some sign whether to go on.

"He used to say to me, 'Edith, I'm crazy, I know I'm crazy, but I believe that somewhere out there there's a civilization so advanced that they'll know how to cure her.' And that was his search. He'd try to go every place a UFO was spotted, and I'd—I knew how much he was suffering—and I'd go with him whenever I could. I don't think he ever really believed it, though; I know I didn't. But he didn't want to give up the hope, and I didn't want to be the one to make him give it up."

I was trying to think of something to say that made sense, that wasn't trite.

"So if anyone," she said, "says anything about him being crazy, feel free to tell them. I want you to tell them."

I nodded.

"That's—" But she'd begun to cry. "That's just one of the reasons I know, I absolutely know, he would never kill himself. He would never, ever leave us—not poor Janie, not Martha and Sally. And not me. He would never do it."

And this time, staring at her, I knew that nothing would ever shake me from it either.

Chapter Fifteen

It was ten of four when I left her house, but I wasn't about to go back to work, to that gloomy building, to that gloomy floor. I was so filled with what I'd learned about Mr. Glennie. The novel. My God, an author and never said a word about it. And a gregarious neighbor who bowled and "knew everything." And the crazy, as even he called himself, looking to the universe for the miracle to make his Janie whole. And then the poor guy I knew about, who so loved books and took all that shit . . .

And as for Mrs. Glennie, I thought of her with a special kind of sadness. I wondered if she would ever regret confiding in me, a stranger, but then again not so much of a stranger as I'd thought: rather the "Thomas" they'd often talked about, perhaps as someone young they related to from the past. Although I'd indicated I would, I could never see myself telling anyone in that building why he'd been reaching out so desperately to space. She assumed it would win sympathy, understanding, but I was sure it would only make him crazier to those pricks.

And in the morning as I approached the building, it was no easier walking in there. I just didn't want to see those people. A woman who worked on another floor, whom I'd often seen but never spoken with, was standing by the elevator. She looked at me, and after I nodded hello she said, "I don't know if you heard about it but they found that poor man's briefcase."

"Where?" I was so startled that the word just shot out.

"Somewhere in the river. I just heard it on the car radio. I think near one of those little islands."

The door to the elevator was opening. I couldn't wait until she got in so I could ask her questions. Then as soon as I followed her: "Did they say anything else?"

"All I remember is just that it was closed. And that it just contained papers. That poor man," she said with a shake of her head. "He seemed very nice. And very shy. But he always said hello."

"Yes, he was a nice guy."

Mrs. Dwyer looked up at me from her desk as I approached. She nodded.

I said, "Did you hear about the briefcase?"

"Yes. On the radio. While we were having breakfast."

"Did they say when they found it?"

"Yes. Sometime yesterday."

I wondered whether before or after Detective Orster had been over. But what difference did it make? He probably wouldn't have mentioned it anyway.

I walked with a heavy feeling into my cubicle. In a way it was as if he'd died all over again. Mrs. Dwyer had put some medical magazines and a couple of manuscripts on my desk. I didn't feel like even glancing at them. I kept thinking of that satchel floating in the water, like a disembodied part of him. I began picking up the magazines but after a glance at a few pages set each one down. I couldn't maintain any interest in them. I found myself wondering if they would hire someone for Mr. Glennie's job, then if they'd offer it to me. I wondered if I even the hell wanted it. But mostly my thoughts kept going back to him gone, and if he'd plummeted from one of the bridges or had walked into the water carrying that satchel, as locked to him by his fingers as if he were still at work. But the images were quickly replaced by that of a killer wanting to get rid of every part of him. And then Frederick Meehan was standing in front of me.

He was holding some papers in one hand, which made me realize for the first time that he almost always carried around a paper or two: it was as if he didn't want you to think you were the only reason he'd walked all this distance from his office.

Gruffly: "You didn't come back."

For an instant, but just an instant, I didn't know what he meant. "Yes, Mrs. Glennie asked me to come back to her house."

"You got a job here, got work to do." Then, as though he'd made his point: just watch yourself if I ever have to repeat it, "You're taking over. All right?"

Again, for just an instant, I wasn't sure what he meant. "Yes. Sure."

"We'll see how it works out. You should know enough." And with that he turned and left.

But now that he was out of there, I wasn't sure at all. I was too deep in the gloom and puzzle of Mr. Glennie's death to want to even think about replacing him. And then there were parts of his job I didn't know how to do because he'd never shared them with me, surely out of that fear of me even though Mrs. Glennie claimed he liked me. But most important I wanted no part of them, of production, the laying out of the books, selecting fonts and size, the buying of paper, all the things that Mr. Glennie did himself so that Meehan could keep our little section running as cheaply as possible: cheaper than if the regular production people in the building did them. I wanted my job to be, in addition to acquiring books, strictly editorial.

Yeah. Good chance.

But hatred began fueling me, hatred of that son of a bitch in the front office: that and all those thoughts of Mr. Glennie always bent over his desk in there, and, Christ, even still gripping that satchel as he walked from here to his death.

I walked up to Meehan's office. I ignored his secretary and stood in his doorway until he looked up.

"Can I have a few minutes of your time?"

"Now?" As if that's not why I was there.

"If you can."

He watched as I approached his desk. I didn't feel even a little tense. It was amazing.

"Mr. Meehan, I was thinking of the best way I can build up the department. I'm good at acquiring manuscripts. And I know what to do with them when I get them. But I'm concerned about the time I'll have to put into production, which you know I've never done."

His eyes narrowed a little. And I felt myself growing nervous for the first time.

"I'm concerned," and then I said it so stiffly I couldn't believe it, "because it can keep me from really exploiting my strengths."

"Well, so what? What about it?"

"I'm asking if the regular production people can handle it. I think it will pay off."

He grunted softly, looking at me. But he said nothing. Then, almost imperceptibly, he shrugged his thin shoulders. It took me a few seconds to realize that it was his okay. And this came to me only because he immediately turned his attention to some papers on his desk. I stood there looking at his bent head.

"Thank you."

He glanced up only long enough to nod. I walked out, feeling exhilarated, light. A weight had been taken off the job, and me. But soon it was as if someone were looking on to make sure I wouldn't feel good for long.

Almost the instant I got back to my desk the phone rang.

"Tom, this is Edith Glennie."

"Oh, hello." Then, awkwardly, "How are things going?"

She didn't answer that. Instead she said, "I just want to say I feel awful for laying so heavy on you. It wasn't right. That's all I want to say. It's been on my mind. And I want to apologize."

"Apologize? Apologize for what?" Just about all I could think of at the moment was here I'd just been given her husband's job.

"You know. You're being kind. I've just been feeling awful about it."

"No, don't. Please."

"I just feel awful. I didn't know you. Really hardly know you. But it's like I do."

I was going to say, "Mrs. Glennie," but remembered I had no door to shut and I didn't want Mrs. Dwyer, anyone, overhearing what I wanted to say. "Can I call you right back on a different phone?"

"Of course."

I went into Mr. Glennie's office and closed the door. I had been in his office twice since his death, just for a few minutes and never with the door shut, which made a strange difference. Dialing her number, I stood with the receiver to my ear.

"Yes, Tom," she said before I even said hello.

"I don't know why I didn't tell you this but I want you to know that a detective was over my place the other evening. He wanted to talk to me."

"Oh? What did he say?"

"He just asked some routine questions. But he did tell me what he said he told you, that they don't think Mr.

Glennie was—murdered."

"Yes, that's what they did tell me," she said bitterly. "But they're wrong, they're wrong!"

"Well, I just want to tell you that I really and truly feel you're right."

"Oh Tom."

"I didn't know him all that well but I just can't see it otherwise. And—I just want you to know."

"Thank you, Tom. Thank you. I've—I've felt so alone, like all I can do is shout out a window."

"Well, instead of that you call me."

"Oh Tom," she said again. Then, after a long pause, and pleadingly, "But who? Tom, I don't think he ever made an enemy in his life. Not one. Ever."

Troy Roper showed up just before noon. His blond, grinning head said, "Well," dragging it out. Then, "Congratulations."

"Thanks." But part of my mind was still back on that call.

"I'm telling you," he said, which made no sense, then started to leave but then came back. "How about lunch?"

I looked at him. "Fine." It would be our first.

Two women were on the elevator when we got on. One was the editor-in-chief of the trade division, a rather homely but handsomely-groomed woman in her late forties whom I'd seen several times but never met. Roper began chatting with her immediately, then when we got off asked if the two of them would like to join us for lunch. Only she said yes— they'd both been going off separately—and it was only then that Roper introduced us—"Corinne, Tom. Tom," he explained, "has taken old Sam Glennie's place."

"Oh?" She held out her hand. "That was a terrible

tragedy. Terrible. But congratulations. And good fortune."

"Thank you."

As we walked on, with no restaurant in mind yet, she said, "I only had one real conversation with him. He had quite a mind. And he wrote an excellent novel. He was very shy about it, I just about had to pry it out of him. But it was excellent—a mystery, you know. Did either of you read it?"

I said, "I just learned about it after he died."

"I never got around to it," Roper said.

We went to a small French restaurant, where she ate delicately of a salad. She talked about a novel they'd just purchased, which was by a relatively unknown though this was his third novel, that had bestseller "written all over it."

"God knows we need one," she said. "But now I've got to get the money to promote it. I hope I can shake enough free."

I thought she might look down on what was now my department, but, if she did, she hid it beautifully. On her own, while we were talking about publishing in general, she said to me, "You're putting out books that have such a limited market that they'd never be published otherwise. It serves a great need, particularly in the medical world."

I said, feeling totally comfortable now, "I've been thinking of something, and I wonder what you think of it. As you know, you send medical manuscripts to us, but I was also thinking of novels. Do you get many novels written by doctors?"

She thought. "It happens. Now and then."

"Well, if you come across any that aren't for you, I'd appreciate if you'd send them along. I'd like the chance to evaluate them."

"Oh. Yes, I'll certainly pass that around."

Coming back to the building, I had my first sense of being part of Mallory & Mallory. I even let myself think about when to move into Mr. Glennie's office, though it was something I still had a difficult time lingering on.

Mrs. Dwyer announced to me from her desk, "Dr. Crestman just called. Actually he was calling Mr. Glennie. He didn't know he died. He wants you to call him."

I wondered as I dialed if Tina would answer. She didn't.

"May I talk to Dr. Crestman?"

"He's with patients now. Can I give him a message?"

"Yes. Please. Tell him Mr. Loberg returned his call. I'm with his publisher."

Her whole manner changed; maybe he'd told her to put this through. "I'll see if he can come to the phone."

He could. He said, "This is Dr. Crestman." And waited. It was as if he knew nothing about this.

"Yes, Doctor, this is Tom Loberg. At Mallory and Mallory. I understand you called."

"Yes. Look, I got the proofs. And I finished reading them last night. I can't"—his voice had become almost a whine—"let them go as is."

"That shouldn't be a problem. Make whatever changes you want and send them back."

"No"—he sounded angry now—"I don't want this back-and-forth stuff in the mail. I want it done once and for all."

"Is it something major?" I hadn't even known that the proofs had gone out to him.

"Of course it's major. Why do you think I'm talking? Look, I'm with patients now. Can you come to the house this evening?"

"This evening?" I was suddenly so mad that it was the only thing I could think to say. And I was well aware that he hadn't even mentioned Sam Glennie, hadn't as much as said he was sorry, surprised, whatever.

"Yes. I'll be free about six-thirty. Can you make it then?"

"Yes, I can make it."

"Hold on, my secretary will give you my address."

And I sat there holding a receiver that I suddenly wanted to throw against the wall.

The Crestman home, in a nearby suburb, looked like an old southern mansion, white and with a portico. From the outside it looked as if it had at least ten bedrooms, though I'd heard they had only one child, a son, and even he was away at college. Two Mercedes, one with a caduceus on the license plate, stood in the driveway.

Mrs. Crestman answered my ring. And instead of wearing the pleasant smile I remembered, she looked stern, angry. I said, feeling I had to reintroduce myself, "I'm Tom Loberg."

She nodded slightly but didn't answer. She opened the door wider and let me pass.

"He's upstairs. The room at the head of the stairs." Not her usual "the doctor." He.

The door was open. He was sitting at a large, glossy desk that was cleared of almost everything but the small pile of proofs. My earlier impression of him as looking like Mussolini, from the photo his wife had brought in, was instantly reinforced by the sight of his completely bald head and square jaw. He had stubby arms under a short-sleeved shirt. I was there in a suit and tie, with briefcase.

"Pull up that chair." He waggled a finger.

I drew it next to his desk. I was thinking of Mrs. Crestman downstairs and how often she'd been to the office or had phoned Mr. Glennie to fix this, that, and to make sure about the paper, the print. And now her obvious anger down there, and him taking over.

I thought: he's given her hell about something he saw in the proofs. That had to be it.

103

He said, "Look at this."

At first I didn't know what was wrong with what he was pointing at. It turned out he was objecting that three successive sentences began with "And."

I said, "Excuse me, Doctor, but you wrote it. And we saw no reason to change it. There's nothing wrong with that."

"I think there's plenty wrong with it. That guy"—it was a moment before I realized he was talking about Mr. Glennie—"should have brought it to my wife's attention. Mine. I'm sorry but you people are supposed to be editors."

"Look," you bastard, "it's simple to change."

"I know. I've changed it. I'm just pointing out. But that's small. Look at this."

He went on to make a couple of dozen other changes, all of them unnecessary, apparently still hearing the rules of his grammar school teacher, and he completely rewrote several paragraphs. I didn't dispute any of them. I didn't care. I put the proofs in my briefcase.

"You'll send me another set."

"Of course." But I ain't comin' over again!

Downstairs, his wife raised her eyes from the newspaper she was reading. Perhaps she nodded; if so, I didn't see it. Outside, I flung the briefcase onto the passenger seat. I drove off, fast, a throbbing in my temples. I tried comforting myself with the thought of the order for 40,000 books.

Chapter Sixteen

I called Tina as soon as I got back to the apartment. And even as I was dialing I was thinking how in the hell could she work for that guy.

I answered her cheery hello with, "How're you doing?"

"Good." Her voice had instantly become somber. "But tell me about you," she said, concerned. I had filled her in on everything I knew and felt about Mr. Glennie.

"Not bad. OK. Look, you up to having dinner with me?"

"Of course. But I'll just sit with you. I didn't have any lunch so I had a fast bite on the way home. But listen, I've got news."

"Which is?"

"I've given notice. I'm leaving my job."

"Really?"

"Really. And I've got something else lined up. I'll be working for a home nursing agency. It all happened just today."

"Great. Congratulations. That's great."

"Look, I want to see you."

"Just tell me what time to come over."

"No, stay there, I'll be over your place. I've got a surprise."

When I opened the door for her, she was holding a large flat object covered with brown wrapping paper. I looked at her as she set it down.

I said, "I don't know what you—Let me get a scissors.

If I can find the scissors."

"Just tear the paper. But be careful."

I knew before I began that it had to be a picture of some kind. But until I made the first long rip, I'd forgotten about that painting in the park of the old man surrounded by books. I kept looking over my shoulder at her between each tear.

"You're kidding. You've got to be kidding."

I had it clear now; it stood leaning against the sofa on the debris of wrapping paper.

"You're nuts, you're crazy, you're wonderful! My God."

I went over to her and put my arms around her. I squeezed her hard then let her go, just long enough to look in her face and stammer, "I mean—I mean—Tina, this is too expensive."

"Naah."

"I know, I know. One good holdup covers it."

"Naah, it doesn't have to be a good one."

"Hell, you've just given up your job."

"I told you I've got another one."

"I'm absolutely floored. When did you buy it?"

"The truth? I picked up the artist's card that day and I called him. And I sent him something down and he held it for me."

"Oh God." I put my arms around her again. She pressed her cheek against my shoulder. "You shouldn't have done it but I love it."

"Then you ought to have it."

I lifted her face between my two hands and looked at her and then kissed her gently on the lips. And then I hugged her, squeezed her, then looked into her face again. I put my cheek against her hair. It smelled so clean and good. I had this urge to tell her I loved her. But I didn't. I wasn't one of those guys who could say it easily.

Not then.

She still wasn't hungry and I didn't want anything fancy, maybe just a hamburger and some french fries, so we went to a Burger King. She got the utensils while I got the order; only a small Diet Coke for her.

As we sat across from each other, off by a window by ourselves, she said, "How was your day?"

"Picture perfect."

"That sounds . . ." then she realized it was a pun. "That was very clever," she conceded, smiling. "Now how was your day? Really."

"Oh. Really. I saw your boss. Your former boss, I'm happy to say." She waited, questioning me slightly with her eyes.

"Something's going on in that house. First of all, up till now he's had nothing to do with the book, but now he's taking over the whole thing. And his wife, she's out. And she looked ready to kill. They had to have had some big battle."

She looked about to say something but didn't.

"And what a nitpicking jerk he is. He might be a mighty good doctor but I'd say he's also a horse's ass."

"He is a good doctor," she said softly.

"I'm sure. But of course I'm not in the best of moods myself, so you can take off a few points for bias."

"Anything more happen today?"

"Well, yes. I was handed Mr. Glennie's job."

She looked as if she were going to say congratulations, but instead said, quietly, "You're having a problem with it. I can understand that. But you shouldn't, you know."

"I know that. And I won't. Anyway, Mrs. Glennie called again today. It's rough, poor thing. She kept apologizing for laying it on me. Her words."

"Poor woman."

"And again it was he was murdered, he didn't have any enemies but he was murdered. She sounded almost happy when I said I thought so too."

"Well, it's the support she's not getting, maybe from anyone." She looked at me. "Tom—" she seemed hesitant—"can I ask you something?"

"Of course."

"Please don't be angry. But are you all that sure?"

"I'm not angry. Why should that make me angry? But whoever said I was sure? It's just what I feel. Strongly. Even though he was a guy I don't think ever as much as offended anyone. And if he was having, say, an affair—anything's possible but in his case I—don't—think—so."

She reached over and put her hand on mine. She looked in my face as she squeezed it. I squeezed back.

Outside it was dark; almost eight-thirty. We walked back to my place, holding hands. I thought I might smoke some pot, though I knew she didn't anymore. But by the time I got there I didn't want it; in fact I had cut down so much that I hadn't touched it in months.

All the lights on, we admired the placement of the painting; I'd had to go out and buy picture hooks.

"I still say you shouldn't have put out all that money."

"Come on," she said, "don't you think you deserve it?"

"Oh, that's another story."

She laughed and I caught her by the waist, turned her around and kissed her. Soon she was watching as I unfolded the sofa bed. Standing, we helped undress each other, but it became so frantic and clumsy that we had to back off and do it ourselves. Then, holding on to me, she sank with me onto the bed. And this time, afterward, looking her in the face, one arm draped over her, I said it.

"Tina sweetheart, I love you. You know that? You know I love you?"

She lifted herself and hugged me. I thought, and later I knew for sure, that she was crying against me.

"I love you too. Tom. Oh God I love you so much."

Chapter Seventeen

Two days later I moved into Samuel Glennie's office. That first day I couldn't shake off the feeling that I was wearing a dead man's clothes, but by the second day it had begun easing away. Still there were times I would find myself thinking of him in the way I remembered him best: hunched over the desk as he worked, or just hunched in his chair as he read a book during lunch.

Meehan came in the second day, holding papers as usual. He glanced around as though I might have made some forbidden change in the place.

"Just want you to know this means you'll be getting a raise." It came out grumpy, of course. "Don't know how much yet."

"Thank you. I appreciate it."

"Well, we'll see if we both appreciate it. Let's see if you can do the job."

I watched as he walked out. He was such a mean pain in the ass, even when he was so-called nice, that I almost smiled despite my hatred of him. I even thought of a bit of sick humor: that I'd prefer that Mr. Glennie was murdered than thinking that this job, now mine, had killed him.

I really didn't think much more about Samuel Glennie during the next two or three days. But I did think of him; I mean, the memory of him would come like a sting, sharp but fast-fading, mostly in the middle of something I'd be doing at the office. And I was quite busy. I was going over the papers of the asthma symposium, was trying to acquire a "history of the emergency services" at a famous midwest hospital, and was going through a small pile of manuscripts, including one on 17th century therapies that Corinne had sent down as a rejection from Trade. And I saw Tina every evening. Once we went to her house, to pick up a lamp table she wanted, but I knew she wanted her parents to meet me in a way that would seem spontaneous. They hardly seemed impressed; they sat, for the most part, graven while we talked of—what? I don't remember, maybe because my heart never quite settled down. But I remember saying on the drive back, "Well, my charisma really got to them," and her laughing and saying, "Please don't take that to heart. I guess we shouldn't have dropped in on them just like that." And of course I remember her asking did I mind driving her to church, that she just wanted to go in for a few minutes.

I looked at her, surprised.

"This really has nothing to do with you and my parents," she said with a little smile. "And I really don't do this often. In fact, not at all anymore. But it's just something I want."

"Sure."

She directed me through several miles of city- and then outlying-streets, to this large Greek Orthodox church, St. George. She'd obviously known she was going to do this because she'd brought along a little white kerchief which she pinned to her hair. The church was almost empty; there was no service. I kept glancing over at her as she sat for a while, then watched as she knelt and closed her eyes for a couple of minutes. Then she stood and we left, all in silence.

Meanwhile, I was searching the newspapers, especially New York City papers, for another editorial job. I wasn't all that sure I would be holding on to this one for long. What's more I wasn't all that sure I wanted to hold on to this one. And most of all I thought I might have a better chance of getting a good job while I was still employed.

Toward the end of the first week after I'd moved into Mr. Glennie's office, his wife called again. I'm almost ashamed to say it but I literally winced, hearing her hello. I didn't want any more heaviness.

"Tom? This is Edith Glennie."

"Oh yes. How are you?"

She didn't answer that. Instead she said, "I hate taking up your time. I really, really do. Believe me. But I don't know who else to turn to there. Mr. Meehan . . ." She didn't finish. But she'd said his name bitterly.

"Just tell me. I'm listening."

"Do you know Mrs. Crestman well? Dr. Crestman's wife?"

"I know who she is, of course. But I don't know her well, no."

"Can I tell you something? Let me tell you something. I-I never really gave this any thought, I mean not in connection with this. I never thought of it that way. But she called our house one night about a week before Samuel . . . before Samuel died. She called our house. I know because I answered the phone. She didn't say who she was, she just asked for Samuel—she asked for 'Mr. Glennie.' I said, 'Who is this?' which I usually never ask, but she didn't answer anyway. Anyway I got Samuel and I left the room. Later, I— Tom? Please, please bear with me."

"I'm right here, I'm listening. Please."

"I left the room and later Samuel came into the kitchen. His face was—was absolutely white. He said, 'She's crazy, she's crazy.' I remember how it scared me and I asked him

112

who and he said, 'Mrs. Crestman! She's crazy!' He was so disturbed all that night. I remember him getting out of bed in the middle of the night. I asked him once what was the matter and he said, 'Nothing. Nothing,' as if he was angry at me, 'she's just crazy.' But he never brought it up again. He never as much as brought her up again. And I just—I didn't forget, but I couldn't see it fitting into this. But what I'm asking you, what I'm calling about, would you know anything about what was going on?"

"I have no idea. None."

"Anything about her. Anything about her husband. That book."

"No, I don't."

"Oh. I thought . . . I don't know what I thought. Look, I'm sorry to bother you."

"No, you're no bother."

Softly: "I'm sorry. I'm really am."

And with that she was gone.

I sat there for a while in a kind of daze. I hadn't told her about the anger I'd seen in Mrs. Crestman and how Dr. Crestman had replaced her on the book; hadn't told her because though Mrs. Crestman might indeed be "crazy," what I saw in that house looked simply like a family feud, and I wasn't about to get involved. And with a job as new and uncertain as mine I wasn't going to help Mrs. Glennie make wild accusations against a woman whose husband was my major client.

But I didn't try to stop myself from thinking. I kept looking over at the two green, metal file-cabinets in the far corner of the office. I went over to them and pulled open the drawer that contained the "C's." I pulled out the file, a thin one, tagged CRESTMAN.

I began flipping through it, looking for something that might possibly explain the phone call to Mr. Glennie. Mrs.

Glennie had said it had been about a week before he disappeared, so say the twelfth of August. And a letter dated August 15 grabbed me. It was to Mr. Glennie from Mrs. Crestman.

It was handwritten, on her stationery. It said, simply:

Dear Mr. Glennie,

I just want to apologize again, and to let you know that I will be forever grateful if you would or already have destroyed it.

Sincerely,
Allie Crestman.

I stood there staring at it, wondering what in hell she had wanted him to destroy. And why. And if he'd done it.

Mrs. Dwyer walked in just then, startling me, as if she'd caught me spying there at the open cabinet. She placed some mail on my desk and left. I took the Crestman file over to my desk to go through it again, more carefully. But there were only a handful of things to look at—carbons of Mr. Glennie's letters to the printer, to the jacket designer, the binder; bills from them; and only one other letter from Mrs. Crestman, this one changing the wording of a heading. But nothing that looked in any way threatening, dangerous, or embarrassing. I could only think he had destroyed it, whatever it was.

I pushed the file away from me on the desk, wracked by questions. What could it have been? And what about the call from her that had Glennie saying, "She's crazy, she's crazy"? Why hadn't he told his wife what she'd said? And his destroying something—what could have been so secret that he didn't confide in her? And then—and then there was Mrs.

114

Crestman, with her anger at her husband, and his taking over the book.

But even that wasn't all.

I remembered, as if it were an image slowly forming, Mr. Glennie coming in my office that time and asking awkwardly, out of nowhere and without explanation, if I'd heard "from anyone"—from Mrs. Crestman, it turned out. Why? Was he trying to find out if she'd revealed to me . . . what she had to him?

Chapter Eighteen

It was hard to work, and yet I had to finish editing the asthma book that day and give it, with photos of the several authors, to Meehan for a final going-over. It was a struggle to concentrate; Mr. Glennie kept intruding. His death had unpeeled a lot of the man, but even now that I had come to know and understand him more I felt almost as distant from him as before.

I turned the finished manuscript over to Meehan about four o'clock. He was in my office no more than ten minutes later. He held up one of the photos.

"You want your job or not?"

I just looked at him.

"You want it or not?"

"Of course I want it."

"Look." He came closer to me with two pictures and dangled them above my desk. "This is not Dr. Kornfield, this is Dr. Brister. You labeled them wrong, and the instructions are clear!"

I shook my head bewilderedly. "I'm sorry."

"Sorry isn't enough. Sorry isn't enough."

I took a deep breath.

"Sorry isn't enough," he repeated. "I'm just telling you."

He turned and was starting to walk out when, bursting out of me: "Mr. Meehan, can I look at those pictures?" I'd been so sure I had them right that I wanted to see for myself where I'd gone wrong.

He glared at me, furious. Then his hand shot out with

both pictures. I took them and looked at them, then at the backs, at the labels. And after a few moments I saw, as if the sun had suddenly come out, that the labels, as he'd re-pasted them, no longer matched certain pencil markings on the backs.

"Mr. Meehan, these were right before."

"Where? Where?"

I stood up and showed him. He grabbed them from me. He kept looking at them, at the fronts, the backs, the fronts. Then, still going back and forth with them and mumbling, he walked out.

I stood there, my heart pumping, loathing him but as scared for my job as if I'd still been wrong.

The door to my office, meanwhile, was open, had been all this time, and I could see Mrs. Dwyer at her desk, her back to me as she continued with whatever she was doing. It was as though nothing had happened, that she hadn't heard a word. The way she used to do with Mr. Glennie.

I went straight from work to Tina's apartment. She had made the moussaka she had promised, and we ate at the drop leaf table that stood open in the living room. She watched as I began eating, and somehow I sensed it and looked up. "It's great."

"It's not missing anything?"

"Yes, it's missing that you haven't started. Seriously, it's great, delicious."

But she watched me take a couple of more bites before she began. I said, after a good swallow, "Your mother must be a great cook."

"She is good but I really learned from one of my aunts who was a marvelous cook."

"Bless your aunt." I held up a glass of the burgundy I'd

brought, and she held up hers and we touched glasses. "And bless you."

"Ah, that's sweet."

"Tell me about your day."

"It went well. I haven't gone out to any patients yet but I will tomorrow. And how was yours?"

"Oh." I shrugged. I really didn't want to talk about it at the moment, not during that great dinner.

"That good, huh?"

Later, as we stood at the sink with the dishes, she said, "So, how was today? From the look that came over your face . . ."

"It showed?"

"Something showed."

Everything about the day seemed so jumbled that for a few seconds I didn't know where to begin. Then, a hand up against the refrigerator as if to support myself, I told her about hearing from Mrs. Glennie about the mysterious call Mr. Glennie got from Mrs. Crestman, his heated reaction to it, and then about the note Mrs. Crestman wrote to him.

"That's really weird," she said.

"It is that. First of all, you'd have had to know Mr. Glennie to know how really weird it was for him to have gotten so upset by her. He was the meekest, mildest guy."

"But then again he was acting in character if he destroyed something for her."

"That's true. And whatever her call to him was about, it was something he couldn't tell his wife. That I do know. An affair with her? Naah. Glennie an affair with Allie Crestman?"

"I don't believe that for a second," she said, annoyed. "I didn't know him but I know her. No."

"Tell me about her."

"I don't know what's to tell. She always seemed nice."

"Tina, look. She calls the guy. He says she's crazy. She also apparently sent him something she wished she hadn't. Then she apologizes and asks him to destroy it. And then he's found floating in the river."

She frowned, then said with a look of shock, "Are you, are you saying you think she—her husband—had something to do with it?"

"I didn't say that. I don't know what to think. All I know is that this crazy stuff happened right before, about a week before, he died."

"Oh, I don't think—No. No." She shook her head.

"I'm not accusing them of anything," I defended myself. "I'm just saying it's strange, it's weird."

She looked at me. "Come on, let's go in the other room."

We went into the living room, where we sat angled toward each other on the sofa. She lit a cigarette, inhaling deeply.

I said, "Tell me what she's like."

She shrugged. "As I said, she always seemed nice. To me, at least. That's the only way I can describe her." Then she paused. "I don't know if this is fair, I have no real reason to say it, but she also always struck me as, you know, a little neurotic. And it's nothing I ever saw her do. Just that she's real skinny and quick . . . Oh, I don't know."

"How did the two of them get along?"

"As far as I know, all right. I heard that when he first started to practice she used to be his secretary. Then she became his office manager, and then she gave it up when she had their son. And she's very active in charities. You read about her all the time."

"And him, what's he like?"

"I told you—very bright. But a temper, he's got a temper."

"What do you mean by a temper?" I asked quickly.

"A temper. No, not what you're driving at," she said. "He's a 'yell-er.' He loses his temper and he can be a yell-er. But the next minute he can be real sweet. I've seen it over and over. And he's got a great name, of course, in the field. He's on the staff of some journal, he writes for some—"

"I'm wondering why she's so mad at him, why she's not having anything more to do with the book."

"Couples do fight," she offered. "But I've never seen it with them. But then again she was rarely in the office during the time I was there."

"Of course there's an obvious possibility. Doctors, I hear, do have their groupies."

She frowned again, then looked at me sideways as she ground out her cigarette. "Maybe. Who knows? Who knows about anyone?"

She seemed a little tired all at once, and it struck me that I must be coming across as an interrogator. Her body was a little stiff as I drew her to me, but she then loosened and came against me easily. I kissed her cheek, her hair.

"I'm sorry," she said.

"For what? Come on. It was like I was giving you the third degree."

"You come on. No."

She looked at me, then sat back. A frown began to form. "Oh. Speaking of temper. And speaking of the book. You know your old company, Packer . . . ?"

"Packer-Hill?"

"Packer-Hill. I forgot this but you probably know it anyway. Do you know Dr. Crestman asked them to sponsor his book?"

"No." I was astonished. "No, I didn't. God, why didn't you tell me this before?"

"Tom, this isn't our night. I told you I forgot. And when

I'd remember I was sure you knew anyway."

"Don't mind me. Please. It just comes as a surprise." The surprise wasn't that, as one of their "whores," he had gone to the company to finance his book: they gave out all sorts of things to doctors as gifts—books, gadgets, you-name-it. In fact, I had been thinking how to suggest it to him at the beginning but hadn't because he'd become immediately irate at the idea that he would have to finance his book. The surprise was simply that I hadn't known he did go to them on his own.

I said, "Do you know if they did sponsor it?"

"No, I don't. I happen to know he requested it," she went on, "because I typed the letter for him. But I don't know what happened—I had one of those revolving jobs. Anyway, about temper—I know that someone from Packer was in to see him sometime after that. And Dr. Crestman got very angry at him. His door was closed but he was yelling. I just walked away because I really didn't want to hear."

Frowning: "Do you happen to know who the guy is?"

"I remember seeing him there a few times. And I did hear his name, but . . ." She thought, then shook her head. "I'm sorry."

I said, "Do you know if he was their usual sales rep?"

"No, I know he wasn't."

"And you have no idea what his name is or sounds like," I tried again.

"No, but if you want I'll try to find out. I'll call one of the girls."

"No, no," I said quickly. "That might get back to Crestman. I'll see if I can find out."

But although that had been a strange incident, I didn't think too much about it at the time. What it did, mostly, was stir up thoughts of the company again: how I'd walked out of there that day for the last time, hurting, worried. I had done a good job but that had apparently meant nothing; the layoffs were you, you and you, depending on where you were and how many heads they still needed there. I thought of the clean, almost sparkling corridors, the L-units, the offices, but mostly the bright, bright lights. The whole place had been so bright, a hundred times more so compared to the shit hole I'd dropped into.

But those lights, oh those lights were to become a lot darker, in a way.

Chapter Nineteen

Late the following morning, after a lot of thought about whether to do it, I went up to Meehan's office. I usually made it a career of avoiding him. He looked at me with the frown I expected. Just a little lift of his head said: What?

I started off with an excuse. "I was speaking to Dr. West-gate"—a retired dermatologist who'd written a memoir of his med school days I was trying to get—"and he'll be thinking it over. I thought you'd like to know where it stands."

"All right." After yesterday in particular, when I'd showed him up, I knew I was far from his favorite person.

I made a move as though to leave, then said, "Oh. I was wondering. Did Packer-Hill, you know the drug company, have anything to do with the Crestman book?"

His head seemed to jerk a little. "No." He didn't ask why; anything. But I felt compelled to say something more.

"Oh. Just a rumor I heard."

I left, feeling awkward as hell; walked back down the aisle past the other offices and cubicles and desks. I was surprised, no almost astonished, that Packer-Hill had turned him down. I wondered why, could only guess that they had tightened up on such things. But it was only when I was at my desk, with Packer-Hill no longer important, that I was fully aware of how tense Meehan still made me. I found myself wondering how the hell Sam was able to handle it.

But it wasn't until a little later that I became aware of something else: that, sitting at that desk and in that office, I wasn't thinking of someone named Mr. Glennie anymore—but, yes, of Sam.

I tried to work but my mind kept racing off on its own. To Sam and Mrs. Crestman, mostly. I could easily see a scenario where he disposed of something he was asked to: that was his way; don't cause trouble, a fuss; especially, don't do or say anything that might jeopardize your job. But what—and this was almost too bizarre for me to even fantasize—had he known that could conceivably have led to his death?

With Mrs. Crestman's anger against her husband, one of the obvious thoughts that stood out, even though shakily, was that it might have something to do with him.

I wished I knew more about the guy. More than that he was a great doctor, wrote for journals, was pretty close to Packer-Hill. There was, for instance, that famous temper. And his yelling at one of their reps. Why? For turning him down on his book?

On impulse I grabbed up the phone to call one of my friends at Packer-Hill, one of the lucky ones who'd escaped the massacre. But then, slowly changing my mind, I sat back.

Asking questions about Crestman: if that got back here, it could trigger a mess, even the end of my job.

I hated myself for that. Although I didn't want to think it—that, goddamn it, I was being Sam. So I did call my friend, Stu Atkins. But I waited until I was back in my apartment where there was no chance of anyone overhearing.

I'd worked with Stu in the general promotion department, and we'd gotten particularly close a couple of years ago, at one of the American Psychiatric Association's annual conventions. The two of us manned a booth on the large, crowded convention floor, where we promoted Packer-Hill's psychotropic drugs. Booths for the various conventions throughout the year took a lot of planning. He and I had also been part of the group that had worked on this one, and it must have taken two months before we came up with a theme and the little perpetual-running slide show and variety of materials that conveyed and elaborated on it. Our theme, I remember, was one of the early ones on marital abuse, and it featured among the booth's backdrops a picture of King Henry VIII. And oh the gifts—the doctors and their wives and whoever else was with them carried around thick shopping bags as they went from booth to booth as if they were in a department store. Then after each day of the convention was over, they could go to any or all of the many hospitality suites the various firms had invited them to during the day.

Stu, a little older than me, had pretty much the same attitude toward all of this as I did: a touch of superiority to the doctors our companies courted in so many ways, but at the same time enjoying our own perks.

A child, a girl, answered the phone.

"Is your daddy home?"

She gave up the phone to a woman. "Hello?"

It was Stu's wife, whom I only knew by name, and she turned me over to him.

"Tom," he came on, "good to hear from you. How are you?"

"Okay." Just about the only time we'd been in touch with each other after I was laid off was when I'd called to tell him I'd gotten a new job. His first question, now, was how was it going.

"Oh. Okay," I said again. And when he didn't push it further, I went on: "Stu, can I ask you something confidential? It's not earth shattering at all, but I wouldn't want it to get around. It's about a doctor."

"Trust me. Confidential. As long as I don't have to keep it a secret."

I laughed. "That's how I like confidential."

"Seriously, feel free. It's confidential."

"Do you know Dr. Crestman? Harvey Crestman? I mean, I knew his name when I was there but I never met him."

"The cardiologist? Sure."

"Do you know him fairly well?"

"Fairly well. Can I ask why?"

"Well, we're publishing a book by him. It's sort of a pseudo-medical thing, more inspirational, I'd say, than anything. And I'd like to know more about him. What kind of guy would you say he is?"

"Crestman? Nice guy's the first thing that comes to my mind. And a real brain. And supposed to be a terrific practitioner."

"I hear that he asked Packer-Hill to finance his book and they turned him down. I was just wondering if they had any special reason."

"Turned him down? Really? That I don't know anything about. But I wouldn't have any reason to."

"I know he gave one of the reps holy hell afterward, and I'm guessing it was about that."

"Huh." He paused, apparently thinking. Then, "I can understand why he'd be upset—you know he's done things for us. But I can understand why we wouldn't do it. Times are changing, the pressure's on drug companies to cut down on the perks to docs and anything that looks like a conflict of interest."

"Stu, I appreciate this. It explains a lot of things."

"Also"—his voice went low, not to be overheard—"we're still having a hell of a time there. We're losing another large one"—I knew he meant a patent on a drug—"and everyone's nervous. Honest to God, just today I was in the men's room with a guy, one of our vice-presidents—I'll leave his name out of this. We're peeing together and he's talking and talking about what's gonna happen, and he's scared to death. And I'm telling you—if things weren't so scary, it'd be funny— he's just about peeing on my shoes."

Chapter Twenty

That night I took Tina to a small movie house in a far section of the city that showed art and foreign films. I drove there with a peculiar sense of relief that I hadn't found anything more on Dr. Crestman. Somehow it deluded me, at least for a while, into thinking that I could let it all go now, could just concentrate on my job while of course still looking for another.

The movie was Fellini's *Amarcord*, as I remember, but mostly I remember the feel and squeeze of her hand in mine. Afterward we had ice cream, double vanillas on sugar cones, which we ate sitting parked in the car by the curb. She'd begun staying in my place overnight, more often than not, and that was one of the nights.

I'd been a little down when I'd first come home from work because I had found two letters in my mailbox, both turndowns for jobs. But everything had lifted completely with Tina, and with it hope in the couple of dozen more resumés I still had out; but now some of the heaviness was back. Watching Tina preparing a late snack I found myself thinking, for the first time with any girl, of marriage. And even more than before, how I mustn't lose this goddamn job.

I thought of it in the dead of night, with Tina sleeping next to me. I'd woke from a dream I couldn't remember but it had left me with a racing heart. As I lay there, unable to go right back to sleep, my thoughts seemed to go all over the place. And then settled on Dr. Crestman, as if I were beginning to recognize what I was running from.

It was a cliché but one of the impressions at least some of us had at the drug company was that those of our docs who were whores would almost rather lose an arm than pay for anything themselves. That went for everything from paperweights we personalized for them, to trips to Honolulu and God knows what else. So all at once I just couldn't see Crestman, turned down by Packer-Hill, simply digging into his own pockets, though they had to be plenty deep, to pay for 40,000 books. What would have stopped him from going somewhere else?

Sam's file on Crestman, I knew, contained nothing about the financing of the book. That hadn't surprised me because I was aware that Meehan handled all financial negotiations. But I kept wondering, longer into the night, what that contract said.

The next day, just to be sure, I sifted through the files of several other books and saw that none of them held contracts either. How, I kept asking myself, though I damn well knew the answer, could Sam have let that happen? How could he have been so afraid? A little later, when Mrs. Dwyer came into my office to pass along some medical journals, I said hesitantly, "I imagine you know, don't you, that we don't keep author contracts in our files here."

"Yes." She sounded equally hesitant, as if not sure what I was driving at.

Although I knew that Sam, and certainly his wife, hadn't trusted her, I did. In fact she had seemed, of late, almost a little motherly to me. I said, "Did Mr. Glennie ever tell you why?"

"No." She appeared reluctant to go. She looked to the open door, then back to me. Her voice low, she said, "One of the girls told me she heard he"—a jerk of her head in the general direction of Meehan—"never wanted us to know—you know, about the dollars." She gave another quick look out there. "She said he gets a percentage."

"I'm not surprised."

"That's why he likes to keep costs low. I was so surprised he hired someone else"—which meant me, of course—"but I think he was really looking for a replacement for Mr. G. But it doesn't explain why he let you give up production. I understand it was cheaper."

"I don't know," I said, "but maybe he's found the Lord."

"Maybe," she said seriously.

"Well, I pity the Lord," I said, at which she looked a little aghast, then started to laugh. She was laughing and shaking her head as she left.

I leaned back in my chair. I'd certainly wondered why Meehan had let me drop production, and so easily. Maybe it was just the first time anyone in this seat had ever requested something, let alone demand it, from him. Maybe he was one of those son of a bitches who are tough, tough—until they're confronted. Or maybe it was just that he felt stuck with me. For a while.

Which brought me back to the contract. Not all contracts, just this one.

Don't be Sam. Christ. Don't be Sam!

I tried to think how to approach Meehan. And some fifteen minutes later as I was walking up the aisle to his office, I still wasn't sure. His door was open but he wasn't there. It was with a kind of relief that I walked back to my office. But within a half hour I was back. He was standing looking out his window down at the street.

"Mr. Meehan."

He turned slowly, then frowned.

"Mr. Meehan, I was wondering about something. I understand Dr. Crestman tried to get Packer-Hill to finance his book but they turned him down. I'm curious if he got anyone else."

"You're curious?" He said it with disdain, and I knew my mistake.

"I think I ought to know."

He kept looking at me. He grunted. "We'll talk later. Got things to do."

He immediately got busy with some papers on his desk. I stood there a short while longer, looking at him. Then I left.

I dropped down at my desk. I was so angry my hand, reaching for a pen, quivered slightly. It was soon almost five. Everyone always left, like kids rushing out of school, at five. Now, though I didn't look at my watch, it had to be five. I could tell by the movement and voices toward the elevator.

"Janquin Foundation."

He was in my doorway. He stood there just long enough to say it. And with a scowl.

He'd said it with as few words as he could bear saying to me. But I knew from occasional newspaper stories that the full name was the Elizabeth and Warren Janquin Foundation. While it wasn't one of the giants, it was highly esteemed for its grants to artists and writers.

I was walking down the hall toward the elevator when something began gnawing at me. But I wondered if I simply didn't remember. I turned and walked through the almost-complete emptiness and silence of the floor to my office. I pulled out the proofs of his book.

Authors generally acknowledge the help and support of a grant.

But here nothing. Nothing.

Chapter Twenty-One

Tina wouldn't be staying with me that night. After work she was to join the girls from Crestman's office for a dinner for one of them who was getting married. The apartment, after all the time I'd lived there alone, felt strangely empty.

She had become indispensable to me. We were perfectly tuned to each other in every way I could think of. Love-making? I couldn't recall a girl I'd ever been with whom I hadn't felt some sense of tension with before we made love. But here we were truly as parts that were one; there was no shame in anything, and always surprise. And she was such a good person. She continued to show up with things for my apartment, sometimes things she could use for her own, or, say, would come in with a package with a new sport shirt because "you shouldn't wear that one anymore." It soon became so understandable to me why she'd had to step away from nursing: it was as though she didn't know how to stop giving of herself. And I was concerned about her now, though she kept assuring me she loved her new job.

I wasn't hungry that night, made myself a grilled cheese sandwich and had it with potato chips and a beer, then realized afterward that I was actually hungry and made myself another grilled cheese, this time with sliced tomato on it. And had another beer. I ate reading the newspaper I'd had since morning but had barely looked at. But for a time I had trouble concentrating. Crestman, I was thinking, was Crestman all around. The bastard didn't want anyone to think that *he* had gotten financial support even though a Janquin was a cachet that writers would die for.

The phone rang about eight, which I thought might be Tina but it was my mother, calling to find out how I was and to share some neighborhood gossip. I hadn't spoken with either of my parents in a couple of weeks, which was about par. I was fortunate in that, active in work and socially, they were no problem to me; backed me in just about everything I wanted to do. And not only had they stopped trying to get me to vote for at least one Republican, but had even stopped asking if I was "seeing anyone."

Tina called soon afterward, from her apartment.

I said, "How did it go? How was it?"

"Good. I had a good time. It was nice being with the girls. We had a lot of laughs."

"That's great. And how was the rest of your day?"

"It went very well. I really feel like I'm accomplishing something. Tom, I'm so glad I went back to it. Can I tell you something?"

"No."

I thought I heard a little gasp. Then she said, with a laugh, "You really got me. But let me tell you. I can tell you now I was scared going back to nursing. But I'm really happy."

"That's great to hear. And I see it. You look happy."

"Ah," she said appreciatively. Then, "It's hard. And there are stresses. But there are such rewards. And I know I can handle it this time."

"I know you can."

"Now tell me about you. Your day."

"Oh." Then I went on to tell her how I'd confronted Meehan about the financing of the book and how he finally let me know that Crestman had gotten a Janquin grant. I even imitated him snapping out the few words.

133

"Oh, he's a real dear," she said.

"Yeah, and I wish it was deer season."

She laughed. "Well, one day you'll go in there and tell him off and pee on his desk."

"I just hope it's not an accident."

"Tom." And again she laughed.

"This guy Crestman's a mystery," I said, serious this time. "And his wife's a damn mystery. I only wish I knew what she had Sam get rid of. And why would she confide in him about anything in the first place? She hardly knew the guy."

"I don't know. I wish I did."

"I know you don't. She's the only one who does. And then there's that fight the two of them obviously had. But as far as you know, they generally got along."

"As far as I know."

"I know I've asked you this, but forgive me. But tell me, what kind of a guy is he? I mean, can you think of anything else?"

"Tom, all I know of him is from the office. And I've told you. A brilliant man. With a bad temper. You know. Tom, we've been through this before."

"I'm sorry." She was right of course.

"It's just—I'm out of that office. And if you want to know the truth, I couldn't wait to get out of there. It was nice seeing the girls again but that's as far as it goes. I'm out of there and I'm happy about it and I don't even want to think about it any more."

"Tina, I'm sorry," I said again.

She was silent. I felt suddenly alone, as if I'd lost her.

"Oh Tom," she said then. "I'm sorry. I just hate to see you unhappy. I—hate to see you working under that terrible man. And I hate to see you worried about—things."

"You mean about what happened to Sam."

"I don't know what I mean," though she knew. And of course was right.

It was as though, somehow, Sam and I had joined souls.

Chapter Twenty-Two

A couple of hours after I got to my office, Mrs. Dwyer brought in a manuscript that Corinne, the Trade editor, had sent down to me. Corinne had written a note with it.

> Tom, here is a ms. of short stories we got over the transom from a Dr. Milligan, a pediatrician in Austin, Tex. We can't even consider it—short stories have always been a hard sell for us. Interested? If not, please return it to him.

I read the first story, then alternated between reading and skimming the others. They weren't all that terrible; far from doctor-author William Carlos Williams; but what was interesting here was that they had a common thread, the experiences of a pediatrician and his patients. My big concern as I kept reading was that he wouldn't go for our kind of deal.

I was almost finished when Troy Roper materialized in the doorway. His mouth was spread in his big-toothed grin. I hadn't realized it was time for lunch, for I was sure he wanted to know if I'd join him. Instead he said, "Hey, what did you do to the Old Man?"

"What do you mean what did I do to him?"

"You tell me. Oh boy, is he mad at you!"

I just stared at him.

He went on, still grinning: "I'd say watch your chair when you sit down. Someone else might be sitting in it."

He stayed there just long enough to see if I had any reaction to that. But I fought not to show anything, though I was boiling. And then he was gone.

That, I assumed, would be the end of his invites to lunch. No doubt I was on the whole floor's shit list again.

But that wasn't the thing that was bothering me. I couldn't remember the last time I felt genuinely nervous, but there was a grinding in me now. Despite myself, I was becoming obsessed with not losing this job. Not now when the turndowns were still coming in—Christ, I wasn't even being asked in for an *interview*. And I was closer than ever, in my head, to asking Tina to marry me.

Meehan had caved in to my giving up production, because he had no one to replace me at the moment. Same for my having the "nerve" to ask about the contract. But he was obviously making angry, threatening noises around him.

Mrs. Dwyer must have overheard Roper, for she was sitting at her desk in the same way she did when Sam would get scalded: bent over, keenly, indeed overly, intense on whatever was on her desk; motherly no more, letting everyone know she was taking no sides.

I wondered what the hell to do. Then, quickly as though afraid I might stop myself, I gathered up the manuscript and carried it to Meehan's office. He stared at me almost from the top of his eyes.

"I've got something very interesting here," I told him. "Corinne Richards sent it down. It's a manuscript from a Dr. Lawrence Milligan. He's a pediatrician in practice in Austin, Texas."

His eyes stayed on me.

"I know we've never done this before," I said, "but I don't see why we can't. Fits right in with the medical. They're short stories about things that happen in a pediatrician's practice.

In fact my concern is we might not be able to get it, he might get an offer—"

"Fiction?" He said it incredulously, his face sour. "Short stories?"

"Yes, but they're on medical subjects. And since we have done poetry . . ."

"Well, we don't do fiction. Altogether different," his only "explanation." "You ought to know we don't do fiction! Where've you been all this time? You've been sleeping?"

"I thought it would be worth a try. It would be like any of the other books. He'd be paying for it."

"We don't do fiction!" And he went back to whatever he'd been doing.

I walked out of there, knowing above my thumping heart that this had nothing to do with fiction, that it was his way of belittling me, of letting me know who was in charge. Even though it could mean losing a decent contract.

Mrs. Dwyer, as though she'd learned to sense these things, never looked up.

I dropped the manuscript on my desk from a height of about two feet, then lowered myself into my chair. I had to fight against charging up there again and telling him what he could do with his fucking job. But I sat there, feeling every hard thump of my heart, then feeling it calm down.

An image had come to me of wild horses.

This is how it happened to wild horses, brought in so high-blooded and magnificent from the range; those bucking, rearing horses finally broken to walk head down. And was this how it had happened in this Dickens-ish hellhole to Sam? And had he even remembered any more how he used to be?

And what of his death?

Again I was back to suicide. Sam finally and completely broken.

But it would be the final payoff, wouldn't it, Christ wouldn't it, if in his meekness his murder came to look like a suicide?

And where, if at all, did the Crestmans fit in?

I thought, as I'd been thinking off and on, of Crestman's grant from the Foundation. How could that shit of his we were publishing pass as art deserving of support from the prestigious Elizabeth and Warren Janquin Foundation? It was so absurd that I felt the need to fill in my friend at Packer-Hill and maybe pick his brain. But as soon as I heard Stu Atkins' hello, I decided not to bring Crestman into it.

"Stu, Tom Loberg. How're you doing?"

"Hanging in there, buddy."

"Stu, you know everything, would you know anything about the Janquin Foundation?"

"Just that I wish I had a grant from them for my novel."

"You writing a novel?"

"No, but if they'd give me a grant I'd try to think one up."

I laughed. "Don't forget to let them know that. Stu, would you have any idea who the Janquins are, how you go about getting a grant from them?"

"No, I really don't. What I do know about them—You know, by the way, that there is no Elizabeth or Warren anymore. They died. Their daughter, I understand, is the main cheese now. How I know, she's married to a guy named Thompson. Quint Thompson."

"Quint? Like in squint?"

"Quint like in squint. By the way, you've never heard his name?"

"No. Should I?"

"Huh. Not surprising, I guess. But joke not, my friend. He's one of those behind-the-scenes guys. He's one of our biggest stockholders."

Chapter Twenty-Three

It was staggering, that Packer-Hill turns him down but then he gets a grant from *that* particular foundation—*that* foundation. A coincidence? It could be, I told myself, sure it could be. But though I knew that fantastic coincidences happen all the time, I didn't believe in them that much. And then there was Crestman's book itself. Art? *That* was art? While God only knew how many tremendous, talented writers couldn't get a penny's support, *Ways to the Heart* wins a grant?

Had Packer-Hill manipulated it?

But that only triggered more questions.

Even if Crestman got that grant with all the pull in the world, what did it have to do with Sam—Sam whose only interests were his family and the quiet almost mole-like reading and making of books; who took all kinds of ridicule to give what he could to his wife and kids; whose only hope, though even he himself called it crazy, was to acquire some miracle of healing from the universe?

And what, most of all, could it possibly do with him floating dead in the river?

I found myself staring at my phone. Then I got up and closed the door to the office and came back. I suddenly wanted to talk to his widow. There was something I wanted to find out, but it wasn't just that: I simply wanted to know how she was, this woman who'd lost not only Sam but his crazy hope for their daughter. Still, I hesitated calling. I was like a lot of other people, I guess, who back away from the troubled or afflicted, from the person with cancer or who lost his job or whatever.

I dialed her number, and she answered.

"Mrs. Glennie, this is Tom. Tom Loberg."

"Oh Tom." Her voice brightened a little. "It's so good hearing from you."

"I just wanted to say hello and see how you are."

There was a long silence. All at once I was a little sorry I called.

"I'm—sorry," she said at last. It was obvious from her voice that she'd been crying. "I'm sorry, but I miss him so much."

I felt stupid. I couldn't think of a thing to say, other than, "I'm sorry if I'm upsetting you," and that was stupid too.

"No, no, no. I'm so glad you called, Tom, honestly. And tell me. How are you?"

"Okay. I'm doing all right."

"Good. I'm glad to hear that." She paused. "You know, I-I've been thinking about you. Please don't take this wrong, but can I say something?"

"Of course."

"Please don't take this wrong. But—you're young and I just want to say it. It's almost like you're my son. But—Tom, don't let them do what they did to him. What he let them do to him. I know it's a job and you must need it but try not to let that happen."

I couldn't speak for a moment. It was as if a lot of stings were rushing to my eyes.

"Don't," she pleaded, "be their whipping boy."

"I won't. I promise you that."

"I know I'm butting in. But I had to say it. And I used to say it to him. I-I knew it was because of us, and I used to tell him, I used to say Sam, we'll get along. But he used to make believe he didn't know what I was talking about. Like everything was okay there. But I knew how he hurt."

"I won't let it happen." It was still all I could think to say. Then, after several moments, I said hesitantly, "Can I ask you something?"

"Of course."

"It's about work. Would you happen to remember if Mr. Glennie ever said anything to you about Packer-Hill? The drug firm?"

"Packer-Hill? No," she said slowly, "but let me think." A long silence followed. Then, "No, I'm sure not. I'm positive. No, why?"

"It's really not important. I'm just trying to clear up something in one of our contracts."

"No," she said again. "I never heard him mention them. No."

We both seemed to be struggling now about what to say next.

"He was murdered, Tom." But her voice was strong as she said it. "I believe you when you told me you believe that too. But I'm sure you're also tired of me saying it—everyone is."

"No, I'm not, Mrs. Glennie. I swear."

"Someone"—she went on as if she hadn't heard—"put him in that river. I know it, I know, I know it. He would never, ever, ever do this to us."

I could only take a deep breath.

"But Tom, can I tell you something? You knew Sam. You knew what he was like. Can I tell you a fantasy I have of him? I have this fantasy of him looking down at me. And even smiling a little. And do you know what he says to me? He says, 'Edith, let it go. Just let it go.' "

★ ★ ★ ★ ★

It stayed with me all day. *Edith. Let it go. Just let it go.* I could even see the poor of son of a bitch saying it. *Let it go. It's ok. No fuss. I'm all right.* It even kept coming to me out in our small park where I sat with Tina after dinner. It was still bright out, the weather just right, and parents were out with their children, and lovers walked hand in hand, and the elderly watched from benches, and pedigree dogs strained against their leashes, and a cop strolled.

Just let it go.

I had things I wanted to tell Tina, and to ask her, but after our last conversation I felt I could talk to her about anything but the Crestmans. I'd known, of course, that she'd been eager to get out of that office but I hadn't known how badly. But after a while I couldn't hold back. I mentioned the grant from the Foundation.

"There had to be," I said, "some pull used there."

"It certainly does look that way."

"Tina, do you know of anything Crestman is doing for Packer-Hill at the present time?"

She thought. "No, I don't. I really don't."

"Do you know who might?"

"I don't know. I would have to ask around."

"But you typed his letters, didn't you?"

She looked at me, suddenly angry. Her hand, which had been in mine, pulled away. "Are you saying I'm not telling you the truth? And anyway don't you listen to anything I say? I wasn't his personal secretary. I just helped out now and then. I typed. I had other duties. There was a lot of typing."

"Tina, I wasn't criticizing you. I was just curious. Teen," I added weakly, "you should have heard Sam's widow. It's so damn sad."

She looked at me. "I'm sorry. But like I said, I hate to see

143

you so upset. And I feel you're just going round and round."

"All right, let me just ask you this." What had seemed simply an incident before was now taking on something of the sinister. "You heard Crestman yelling at someone from Packer-Hill."

"Yes, I did. And this is what I mean by just going round and round."

"And you say he wasn't their usual sales rep."

"That's right. Their usual sales rep," she repeated quietly, "is a woman. At least she was when I was there."

"I just wish I knew his name. I haven't even tried—"

"Look," she said quickly, standing up. And when I rose with her, she took my arm. "I'm going to call someone. I don't know if she'll know, but let's try."

We walked over to a pay phone and she inserted coins I gave her. She was on the phone for about five minutes, mostly with her back to me. When she turned, she said, "All she could remember was that it was an unusual name, like . . . Featherly. Only it wasn't Featherly."

We stood there, looking at each other.

"It does ring a bell," she said. "I did know it . . . I did . . ."

We began to walk on, back into the park. We were deep into it when all at once she stopped, lifted her arms in a kind of glee, and grinned at me.

"Ah," she said. "Featherman. Like Letterman. Featherman." Her hand took mine again.

"Now," she asked, "can you enjoy the park? A little?"

Chapter Twenty-Four

I remembered Featherman well from Packer-Hill, though I had never met him, and was surprised I hadn't made the connection. He was one of those upper-management people you would see around, who held a fairly high position in the company but you were never sure what it was. The same with his name. I used to hear him called Ed, but I'd never given a thought to whether it was Edward, Edwin, Edgar or what.

What I remembered mostly was a usually-smiling guy with a crewcut, at times one of the group of executives who would come into the company cafeteria, work-like in rolled-up-sleeve white shirts and ties, and carry their lunch trays like everyone else and sit at one of the regular long tables, though it was tacitly reserved and as though behind glass.

But what was his connection with Crestman? And why the yelling at *him?*

The first thing I did when I got to the office was try to learn something more about him. I made a fast call.

"Packer-Hill Laboratories. Good morning."

"Good morning. I need some help. I'm writing a letter to your Mr. Featherman but I don't know his title. I'd appreciate it if you would help me."

"Just a moment, please." The operator left, then came back on. "He's Associate Director of Corporate Affairs."

"Oh, and his first name, please."

"It's Edward."

The receiver down, I wondered what that title meant—

they had so many goddamn titles there. And it could mean a lot of different things. I started to call back, this time to talk to my friend Stu Atkins, but slowly placed the receiver back on the cradle. It was why I hadn't called him in the first place: I'd asked him enough questions, was hesitant about pressing him too hard.

Mrs. Dwyer came in shortly and placed some letters and a package that apparently held a manuscript on my desk. The mail was junk, all from vendors who assumed Special Projects was still doing its own production. I ripped the wrapping paper off the package. The letter accompanying it was from a retired surgeon, and the manuscript was the story of his experience as a naval medical officer in World War II. We'd lost one memoir on the war, but that one was army and maybe we'd have better luck with navy. I flipped through it, occasionally stopping to read, then on impulse pushed it away and reached for the phone.

"Packer-Hill Laboratories."

I said, "Mr. Stuart Atkins, please."

His secretary came on. "May I tell him who's calling?"

"Yes. Tell him it's Tom Loberg."

He took it immediately. "How's it going, fellow?"

"Good. Good. Yourself?"

"Good. But if you'll wait till I close my door I'll tell you the truth." But he said it as though with a smile.

"Stu"—I was apprehensive—"I've a question about someone there. Can I ask if—"

"Wait, wait. Give me your phone number again. I'll have to call you back."

I gave it to him, and he called about five minutes later.

"I'm calling from a public phone here," he explained. "This place has become nutty and I don't trust anyone."

"I'm sorry I'm putting you to all this trouble."

"Cut the crap. It's too late. Now tell me."

"Ed Featherman. Can I ask you? I know his title there but what does his job involve?"

"Him? Oh . . . It's a fancy title for keeping docs happy. And the politicians happy. A lot of troubleshooting, making nice. As for him—Remember that guy I told you about almost peed on my shoes?"

"This him?"

"No. No. But what I'm saying is that it could have been him. Nervous. Afraid, you know, the company's going under. Or more likely will be taken over. He's been here since he was, I think, two, and now he's scared. Well, everyone is, a little. A lot."

I took a deep breath. "Stu, remember I told you about Dr. Crestman giving someone from your company hell? Remember my telling you?"

It took him a few moments to recall it. "Okay."

"And this was after you people turned Crestman down about the book?"

"His book?" He'd forgotten about it. Then, "All right."

"And remember I asked you about the Janquin Foundation and you said the husband of someone there is one of your biggest stockholders? Well, Janquin gave Crestman a grant."

He didn't say anything this time.

I said, "Featherman's the guy Dr. Crestman gave hell to. So I'm curious about what his job actually is, if he could have the kind of influence to get Janquin to—"

"Wait, wait, wait," he cut in. Then, "You know something? You wanna know something? I must be the dumbest guy in America."

The sudden anger in his voice surprised me.

"Make that the world," he went on. "Make that the whole fucking world. It's just dawned on me that not only are you pumping me but I'm acting like a complete asshole. I'm even callin' you on a pay phone. What an asshole!"

"Stu . . ." though I didn't know what I was going to say.

"Are we buddies?" he demanded. "We're not buddies. We just know each other. But you're pumpin' me and I'm lettin' you! This is my job, you're not my job! Go to hell, hear me? Go the fuck to hell!"

And the phone went dead against my ear. And for long moments I just sat there, feeling rotten, feeling stupid, feeling totally naive—and feeling even exposed, in a numbing way, to danger.

Tina's mother had invited us for dinner that evening. Both her mother and father were much friendlier to me, and I felt a lot more comfortable with them, though there still seemed to be a space between us through which they were feeling me out. They appeared to enjoy watching me eat and occasionally asked if I'd ever had something or other before. I had: Greek salad, of course, and even the beef stew which I'd never known was called stiphado. The father left early for the pizza parlor; and when Tina and I were at the door, about to leave, her mother said to her, "I'll call you later on," which we knew was her way of saying stay at your own place. But Tina had no intention to.

As we were driving, the radio on, Tina turned it off and looked at me. "Tom, tell me. What's the matter?"

"What do you mean?"

"Your face, your expression. You were fine at my house and now everything's changed. What's wrong? Is something wrong?"

She was right. I had managed to push Stu Atkins out of my mind while at her house, but that whole ugly episode had rushed back. I told her about it.

"The thing is," I said, "I don't blame him. I was just using him."

"Are you kidding? Come on. It's not like you were pretending, like you were lying to him."

"I know but I feel lousy about it."

"You really shouldn't."

We drove on in silence. She came out of it after a while, to say, "Look," and her hand came on my knee, "I've just thought of something. I don't know if it'll help or not but I've just thought of it. I don't know why I didn't think of it before. You know, my old boss"—it was as if she didn't want to even say Crestman's name any more—"doesn't only work out of that office. He's at the hospital at least three mornings a week and he sees patients there. He may be doing something for Packer-Hill there. I don't know."

"You never worked there?"

"No. I don't even really know the staff except for talking to one or two on the phone."

I pulled the car over to the curb but left the motor running. I said, "Those you know, do you know them fairly well?"

"No. Not really. But I was still thinking of asking them—you know, about it."

"Tina, I don't want to put you through that."

"I'll try to figure out a way. I'll see. I don't know."

I reached an arm out to her and she let me enclose her in it. She turned her face up for a kiss, then put her head against me.

"Tom, I love you."

"God, how I love you."

"I'll do anything for you. I just want you to be happy."

"Oh, Teen." I lifted her face and kissed her again. And this time she swung her free arm around me and squeezed me with all her strength.

★ ★ ★ ★ ★

Tina called me about one o'clock the next afternoon.

"Tom, I've got something but what an ordeal."

"Tell me."

"I just hung up. Wait a second." She paused to catch her breath. "I called this nurse—she's his right hand at the hospital. I'd spoken her to her before, about two-three times altogether. I asked—you know—if he was doing anything for Packer and she tells me but then it's like she suddenly thinks of something and she asks why. I made up some shitty story about my mother having a bad heart, and then she says, 'You don't work for him any more?' And when I said no she almost had a fit."

"Oh Tina, I'm so sorry."

"She began yelling—my heart's still going a mile a minute. Anyway, he's doing clinical testing on one of their drugs. It's supposed to prevent heart attacks during and after surgery. But it hasn't been approved yet. That's all I know about it."

"Did she give you the name?"

"No. And I'll be honest with you, I couldn't wait to get off the phone."

"Oh Tina."

"Look, I've got to go back to work."

"Sweetheart, thanks."

I put down the phone, but for a few minutes my hand refused to relax its grip on it.

Even if this held the answer, what in God's name could it have to do with Sam and that goddamn book?

Chapter Twenty-Five

I quickly picked up the phone again, this time to call another friend back at Packer-Hill, the only one I could think of I could really trust. Jack Trivers. He was in the public relations department, which was somewhat different from general promotion: while they publicized the company to the public, we publicized its products to the doctors.

A new drug, I knew, had to go through animal studies and then three phases of testing in humans before it could go to the Food and Drug Administration for approval. And I was curious to know where this one stood.

"Jack. Tom Loberg. How are you?"

"My buddy! Good. Well, fair. It's lonely here without you guys."

"You want to hear about lonely," I said. Then, "Listen, Jack. If you can help me with this, fine. If not, fine too."

I explained that I didn't know what the drug I was interested in was called, just what it was supposed to do. And I was wondering if he might be able to find out its name and what phase it was in.

"I wouldn't know," he said, almost solemnly. "Why don't you ask someone in New Products?"

"I would," I said, "but you know how they are." Mighty secretive. Would ask a million questions.

"Well, let me think who to ask. Tell me, it's none of my business but what's it for?"

"We're thinking about publishing something on cardiac

arrest. And I was curious where they were with this one."

"Well . . . let me see what I can see."

I sat back afterward, thinking. Brooding, is more like it. A lot of doctors, not just one or two, investigated new drugs. It wouldn't be just a Crestman, not a lone person, who determined its fate.

Out on the floor, people were going about their work, at their desks or walking in and out of offices and cubicles. They all seemed of a face: dour. It was as though the building itself infected them. I couldn't help think again of Packer-Hill, not just of its brightness but of the way people smiled and said hello and complimented you on your work, and flew you first-class on trips, and gathered and talked at twice-daily coffee breaks. Were *friendly*, for Christ sake, and pleasant and paid well and respected you. And I thought: what am I doing even imagining something sinister from there?

I must have been staring at a corner of my desk, or down, or whatever but with a little shift of my head I was jolted to see Meehan standing just inside the doorway. He stood silently —I had no idea how long he'd been there—just looking at me. Looking.

Then he came forward with that crab-shouldered walk, and wordlessly placed a manuscript on my desk. And left.

It might sound strange, but I felt as if I'd never known until then the depth of my fear for my job. It was as though it had been a veneer before, but now was part of my whole essence. But looking back, I know it was just that each episode, when it came, became compounded with all the others. I despised the feeling and hated myself for it; swore I would never be swamped by it. Still, I drew the manuscript to me quickly, as if an emergency.

It was the former naval surgeon's memoir. My reading of it had concluded that it would need a mammoth amount of editing to get it thoroughly readable, and I had sent it along to Meehan with that comment. My note was back with it. Printed on it in his compressed way were his instructions about editing: 2 days. And this was followed by: Try for it, FM.

I had made up my mind earlier that before I worked on another manuscript I would go into that front office and ask Meehan how he priced the subsidies. It was too soon for that now. First I had to write a letter to the doctor, suggesting how we might publish it; any negotiations would come later.

Later.

But even though it would be later, I just couldn't see myself confronting that fucking Meehan again.

I started dictating the letter to Mrs. Dwyer at my desk. And I got this far:

"Dear Dr. Whetting:

"Thank you for thinking of us as potential publishers of your book, *M.D., Old Salt: The Story of One Doctor's World War II.* Your book casts a unique light, through your experiences, on this particular phase of the war. However, much as we would like to publish it, we are concerned that the market for it is not broad enough at this time. But—"

My phone rang just then. Mrs. Dwyer questioned me with a little raise of her hand if she should take it. I motioned her off.

"Hello."

"Yes. Hello. This is Mrs. Crestman—Allie Crestman."

It came as such a surprise, with her voice so cheerful, that it must have showed on my face. Mrs. Dwyer slowly rose and left, closing the door.

"Yes, Mrs. Crestman."

"I was just sitting here thinking. And I felt the urge to tell you and congratulate you. It's going to be a handsome book."

"Thank you. I know it will be." Meantime, I was remembering how she had barely looked at me in her house, how she'd had nothing more to do with the book. What the hell was *this?*

"I do like the print very much," she said. "And the paper."

"Yes, I thought you made good choices."

"I'm very pleased. And I know the doctor is." He had become "the doctor" again. "Poor Mr. Glennie," she went on. "I'm so sorry he didn't live to see it."

"Yes, that's very sad."

"You were quite close to him, I imagine."

"Yes." If she'd begun worrying, I was thinking, about whether I knew what he was supposed to have destroyed, let her worry.

"Oh, and I want you to know you have one lovely girl-friend in Tina."

Startled, I wanted to ask: How the hell do you know we're seeing each other?—but I stopped myself. "Yes, she is."

"A darling girl. A lovely girl."

"Yes."

"Well . . ." I could see her smiling. "I'll say goodbye to you."

"Goodbye, Mrs. Crestman."

What, I kept asking myself afterward, was that all about? It was so crazy! Was she crazy? One of those people who go back and forth between mania and depression? I was certain how she'd learned about Tina and me; Tina must have mentioned it at that dinner with the "girls" and it was passed on to her.

But the call itself? It made no sense, was totally out of character for her.

But maybe, just maybe, I was beginning to think, that was the purpose. Dr. Crestman's nurse must have told him about Tina's call to her, and he had told his wife. And in a cheery way that made it even more threatening, this was to let us know they knew.

Chapter Twenty-Six

My friend Jack Trivers called the next morning, though it was a Saturday. He'd learned from someone in Research and Development which drug it was.

"I'd have called you yesterday," he apologized, "but I'm sorry, I got tied up."

"Sorry? I appreciate this, you kidding? Thanks."

"Right now they call it LG272. And I hear they have real high hopes for it. In fact some papers have been published on the findings in rats, and then in humans in Phase One. But you know the chances of a new drug working out. Anyway, it's got a long, long way to go. It's still only in Phase Two."

"Thanks again, Jack."

He was right when he said it had a "long, long" road ahead of it. Phase One had to have consisted of studies of its effect on healthy humans. Now, in the second phase, they were doing their first studies in patients, after which they would go onto Phase Three, which involved large-scale studies in patients. And it might take the FDA at least a couple of years after that to decide on it.

Tina, who was putting away breakfast dishes, looked over her shoulder at me. I told her who'd called and what he said.

"I only know one thing," I said. "It looks like a gorgeous day, the sun's out and I want to get the hell out and enjoy it."

"I think you just scared it back in."

"Well, it better come out again. That's a warning."

After about a half hour wait in line for gas, we took off. I didn't care how long or how often I'd have to do it, and or how much the damn gas cost, I just wanted to be driving somewhere out of the city even though neither of us knew where. After we'd been driving a while Tina, who'd brought along a section of the paper called *Saturday*, looked up from it and said, "Do you know where Klentville is?"

"Yes, I always went to debutante parties there."

"Seriously."

"I know of it. What's there?"

"There is," she said, referring to the paper again, "a huge —a *huge*—antique show. Do you like antiques?"

"No. You?"

"Not really."

"Then that's every reason to go."

I had a vague idea where it was: about twenty-five miles from where we were. What attracted us, mainly, was that driving there would take us deeper into the country. The show was held in a large hangar, and the moment we entered we started enjoying it. It was like a carnival, with food booths and masses of assorted things like old tools and TVs and even cowboy chaps, as well as the heavy stuff of antiques. We stayed an hour or so and then had lunch in a so-called family restaurant, then drove on. We went to a lake I knew, looked on from the grass, with the picnickers, at the people swimming, then headed back, perhaps in time for a late afternoon movie.

Driving in the city took us past the eight-story, block-long building that housed Packer-Hill Laboratories. I looked over, as I always did; and, as always, it was with a tinge of nostalgia at the good times there. But this time it wasn't purely nostalgia. It was intermingled with unease.

We didn't go to a movie. We drove first to Tina's parents'

157

house and picked up a little TV, with rabbit ears, she had in her bedroom: she hadn't really wanted it before now. No one was home, and we kissed of course in the silence. We took it to her apartment and then were trying to decide should we eat here or out, when the phone rang. Tina, standing, said, "Hello," and then I saw her eyes widen and her mouth drop open.

She sank to a chair, the phone still clutched to her ear. She never said a word; seemed to rock a little.

I said, frightened, "Tina," but it was as though she didn't hear. I took a few steps toward her, and her eyes lifted toward me. But it was several more moments before her hand came down with the receiver and set it on its cradle.

"Tina, what is it?"

She shook her head, looking at me, then looked away.

"What is it? You're scaring the hell out of me."

She looked at me pleadingly. "No. No. It's all right."

"What is it? Who was it?"

"I—I'll be all right. Just let me . . ."

I waited. She was taking deep breaths. "I'm sorry," she said.

"What're you sorry about? Tina, tell me."

She closed her eyes, shaking her head slowly. Then she opened them. She seemed to be struggling with herself, perhaps over whether to tell me. Then, "It was—That was Mrs. Crestman."

"No. That son of a bitch!"

"It was—it was awful. She kept screaming—'Why did you call? What do you want? What're you after?' And names—she called me such names."

"Why the hell did you listen? Why didn't you just hang up?"

"I don't know." She was shaking her head. Then she

158

looked at me, frightened, when I reached for the phone. She grabbed my wrist. "No, don't! Please!"

"I'm calling that crazy son of a bitch! She and her husband can take that fucking book—"

"No, Tom, don't. Don't do that to yourself. Don't. You'll lose the book. And I'm afraid you'll lose—you'll lose your job."

"I don't give two goddamns."

"Don't. Please."

"Christ, I'm the one who had you call."

"That's all right. That's all right."

I took her in my arms. I felt her body quivering against me.

"Oh, sweetheart," I said.

"I'll be all right. I'll be fine. Just let it go. Let it go."

I held her even tighter. But it was a long moment before I was aware that it was like Sam saying it to me from the sky.

Chapter Twenty-Seven

I couldn't shake that goddamn Mrs. Crestman out of my head. Not that night, not the next morning. Oh, maybe for minutes, maybe for a lot more; but she always kept coming back, that face I could only see now as ugly, sour. And look whom she hurt. Tina, who wouldn't hurt anyone. Tina, who'd at last settled into the work she loved, tending mostly to the housebound elderly. Tina, one of those people who are born to go into nursing and yet are as exposed to its pain as if they have no skin.

I was still thinking hard about calling her, was probably even closer to it than ever, when I heard, "Mr. Loberg," and saw Mrs. Dwyer out at her desk, holding the phone with her hand over the mouthpiece. I could barely remember hearing it ring.

"It's a Mr. Featherman."

I hesitated picking it up. If Stu Atkins had been enraged at me, I could imagine what I was going to get from this guy.

"Mr. Featherman. This is Tom Loberg."

"How are you?" And I immediately relaxed. His voice, even with those few words, seemed to have a laugh blended into it. Which wasn't unusual for the fellows, mostly fellows then, whose job back at Packer-Hill, like his, was purely and simply to coddle the doctors.

"I'm doing fine. Yourself?"

"Good. Look," and this time he gave off a real laugh, "I hear you had our friend Stu blasting off fireballs. Well, he meant well."

"I know he did. I'm very sorry about that."

"Look, I want to talk to you about that. I mean, about whatever you want to know. But first I want to warn you. What's the worse thing you as an editor can hear a friend or neighbor say?"

"Can I borrow . . . ?"

"Naah, that's crap. That's only money. I'll bet you what it is. It's 'I've got a manuscript.' "

I had to laugh. "You may have a point, but actually I'm on the lookout for books."

"Well, have I met the right man. Actually, that's what I'd like to talk to you about. I have a book I'd like to discuss with you. But I promise you I'll answer any question you want. So let's see. Can I see you?"

"Sure."

"What time do you close shop there?"

"Five."

"Oh my. I'd like to make it there today if you possibly can, but I can't by then. I'll tell you what. You free for a little bit after work?"

"That would be fine."

"Okay, a nice bar. One near you, how's that?" He was apparently thinking as he was talking. "Okay," he said then, "here's a nice one. I think about six blocks from you."

I'd never been in the bar he named but I was sure it would be a great one. That's the only kind of place these guys went to.

I was right. It was one of those bars where people come after work with their briefcases, and women smoke long, thin cigarettes. I was a little early. Every stool was taken, so I took one of the few small round tables and ordered a beer while I waited.

It was easy to spot him the moment he walked in and looked around. He saw me standing and came over. He was a good-looking, strong-featured guy, evenly tanned, and with a salt-and-pepper crewcut; probably in his mid-fifties.

He kept looking at me as he shook my hand, firmly. "Sure I recognize you. I didn't from Stu's description, but I used to see you around a lot. Good to see you again."

"Good to see you."

He sat down, briefcase by his leg, and immediately looked around and then waggled a finger in the general direction of the bar. "So," he said to me, smiling, but then stopped as a young woman came over for his order. He ordered Johnny Walker Black, on the rocks.

"So," he said to me again, "you're the guy Stu got all worked up about. What should I talk about first, that or my book?"

"Whichever you want."

His drink came, and he lifted his glass to me. I took a swallow of beer as he sipped.

"My book," he said. "I'm nine chapters into it—I think it'll go at least thirty. Look. This is confidential of course, okay?"

"Of course it's confidential."

"What you've been through at Packer-Hill might be a hell of a reason for me to trust a guy, but it is. It's like having a flying buddy—I'm a pilot—and you just instinctively know what other flier to really trust. Anyway, as you probably know, we're going through the same damn shit. I'm writing a book, been writing a book, on my experiences. I'm not going to spell it out more than that right now. If I'm not there anymore, I'm publishing. And even if I am there, and the right publisher wants this, tells me he thinks it could be a winner, is willing to back it big, I'll go with it anyway."

He looked at me for some sign, and I nodded. I didn't know who was the bigger bullshitter, him or me.

"I'd like to send it over for you to read what I have," he said, "and you can even show it to your people, but that's as far as it goes at the moment. I just want to know what I have, okay?"

"All right." I wasn't so sure any more—not sure at all, in fact—that he actually was bullshitting.

"I'm telling everything I know. I'm holding nothing back. And believe me, I know. Tell me, if you don't mind, how old are you?"

"Twenty-eight."

"You're just a kid—I mean through these eyes. And you look, by the way, I'd say twenty-six. The only reason I asked is that no matter how much you think you know about the business, at your age you can't have been in it long enough to know anything like the whole story. Believe me."

"I'm sure you're right."

"Well . . . Okay, we'll get back to that. Now about Stu. What you were asking Stu. I'll answer any question you want. Any question, that is, that I can answer ethically. I know it concerns Dr. Crestman. He is, incidentally, and I'm sure you know it, one hell of a brilliant doctor. But as a human being— between us—I'm no big fan of his."

I looked at him, trying not to let him see in my eyes what I was asking myself: why are you telling me this?

"First though," he was saying. "I'd like to know why you're asking about him."

I wondered how to tell him, without mentioning Sam's death. "I know you people turned him down for a subsidy for his book. And I was curious that he ends up with a grant from the Janquin Foundation. And I do know about one of your stockholders there . . ."

He smiled, looking at me with a little shake of his head. "What's the big fuss about that? You were in the business. You worked with doctors. You know. Some of them come to expect so much from you, there's no end. It's like everything in their life has got to be free. So . . . if you can't do something outright for them, say that might give something an improper look though it isn't improper at all, you might use a little influence instead. It's no crime. At least not yet. It can eat your guts out, but it's no crime."

He paused, then looked around and raised his finger again for another drink.

"This goddamn business," he said, turning back to me. "Want to see something?" He held out a hand. It was quivering. "It never was like that." He kept looking at it, then said, "I don't mean to pry but tell me what's it like on the outside."

"Not as good as it was. Nowhere near as good."

"Huh." He was still looking at his hand. He made a hard fist, kept it for a few moments, then opened it. The hand was still quivering.

I looked at it, then at his face. I found myself really liking the guy, enjoying his company. But it wasn't until I was heading back to the apartment that I thought how that was his line of work.

Chapter Twenty-Eight

Featherman called the following morning. His "Hi" was enough to reveal the laugh in his voice.

"Tom, Ed. How you doing?"

"Good. You?"

"Good. Real good. Had a great visit yesterday. Hope you did."

"I certainly did."

"Well, listen. Remember that—thing we were talking about? You know? Book?"

"Sure. Of course."

"I'd like to discuss it more with you. I was wondering, any chance for lunch today?"

"Fine. Sure."

"Let's see where. I'll tell you what. You know there are some nice places around here. Would you mind coming up, call me from the lobby? And I'll be down."

"Sounds good."

"Could you make it about a quarter of one?"

"I'll be there."

I hadn't brought my car to work, so I took a cab. It was a strange feeling getting out of a cab in front of that beige-stone building and walking through the entrance: it called back in an eerie way the feeling of having returned from a trip for them, and coming back from the airport. The guard in a blazer with the HP logo over the breast pocket was standing in front of the several turnstiles. I knew him, but he hadn't seen me yet. And I didn't have to go through the turnstiles. The phones were on this side, against one of the walls.

Featherman took the call instead of his secretary.

"Tom. Glad you're here. Look," and with this his voice changed a little; it became almost distressed. "Would you mind coming up? There's a reason. And it may be good for you."

Puzzled, I went over to the turnstiles. The guard obviously recognized me, but only gave me a slight touch of a nod and a smile; it was as though he didn't quite know how to greet the dead. I walked over to the receptionist, who called Featherman's office from her desk to confirm I was expected, and then with a broad smile she gave me a Visitor's badge.

It was a weird feeling being in one of those elevators again. And almost instinctively as I stepped off at the top floor, the executive floor, I glanced over at the wall where company news events and such things as cost-of-living raises were posted on each floor. I felt slightly disoriented, then threaded my way past L-units and offices to Featherman's office. His secretary motioned with a smile to go right in. He was standing in front of his desk, waiting for me.

"Good to see you, lad."

"Good to see you."

He walked over and closed the door. He was wearing the usual long-sleeved white shirt and tie, and the checkered multi-colored pants that were fairly common here.

"Look," he said, motioning me to a chair and then sitting down, "you remember Chuck Olson, of course."

It took me a couple of moments to remember that "Chuck" was really Charles Olson. He was Director of Finance, one of the two executives I'd written speeches for.

"We were at break"—coffee break—"and we started talking about people who'd been let go, and I mentioned I'd

166

seen you and was seeing you today, and he asked did I mind if we stopped by his office for a brief visit. I said sure. Okay?"

"That's fine. Sure."

"Anyway, I want to talk to you first. I've"—and his voice lowered, as if the door were still open—"got what I've written. I have to go over it, and I've got more than half to go. It's here," and he nodded vaguely at a drawer.

"You want me to read it?"

"Yeah, but first I want to talk. Tell me. This should be first-person, like I'm talking, right?"

"I think it would be much stronger, sure."

"Well, that's what I've been doing. That's great. Now, about naming real people. When do I use real names, when don't I? I don't want to be sued the shit out of."

"It depends what you say about them, if you're libeling them. I would say write it with the real names and afterward our lawyers will go over it."

"Great. That sounds fine."

We talked like this for about ten minutes, after which he looked at his watch and stood up. "Let's say hello to Chuck."

Olson, a rather short man with sparse, carefully placed black hair, gave me a strong handshake and smile, and tapped Featherman on the arm. Then he turned immediately to me.

"That was one hell of a speech you wrote for me. I don't know if I ever really told you how much I thought of it."

"You did."

"And it really went over. It really did." He looked at Featherman. "I don't think I'm giving away any secrets when I say the damn company let go some of the cream."

"Noo," Featherman said, almost with a laugh.

"Why I wanted this visit," Olson said to me, "is to find out if you have the time to do others for me. And if you do we can talk about it at the time."

"I'd love to."

"Great. That's all I want to know. And I know others here who are dying—Peter," he interrupted himself, and I turned to see Peter Crain, the executive vice president of the company, standing in the doorway.

Crain said, "Hate to interrupt but just wanted to see if you're ready for chow."

"Sure am." He stood up. "Pete, say hello to Tom Loberg. He was one of our boys. One hell of a writer."

Peter Crain looked at me as he took my hand. "Sure, I remember you," he said slowly. "Remember the face, the name. How're you doin'?"

"We let him go, Pete," Olson said in a singsong way.

Peter Crain looked at me even more intently. When he let go, he just shook his head.

"He'll be doing some speeches for me," Olson said.

"Good. Good." Crain grasped me by the arm as he said it. Then he said mysteriously, "We'll see." And now to Featherman and me: "How about you guys joining us?"

Featherman looked at me quickly, and moments later we were walking together to the door, where standing out in the hall waiting were the president of the company and two other men in white shirts I remembered seeing around. We filed to the elevator, and then into the cafeteria and, with everyone else, along the counters with our trays. Then, as people looked on, we headed toward that long empty table, where I sat with Featherman diagonally across from the president— Scott—and directly across from the executive vice president. And all through lunch, though I couldn't make myself do it and so never mentioned a name, it was Pete and Scott and Tom and Ed and Chuck. And once, in the distance, I saw my friend Stu Atkins, standing and holding his tray, and just staring at me, staring.

Back on the executive floor it was shaking hands all around again, and I went with Featherman back into his office.

"I don't think," he said, "that will do you any harm."

"I enjoyed it." I didn't know what else to say.

"You notice, they don't seem to have a worry in the world, do they?"

"They don't seem to, no."

He looked toward the door for several moments, then turned back to me, frowning. His face, I couldn't help noticing, had become flushed.

"Look," he said, apologetically, "I—I know I'm going to sound like a real horse's ass, but I hope you understand. I've just decided to hold onto the . . ." He nodded toward the drawer. "I've decided to hold onto it a little longer. I want to wait a while. See how things go—you know, here."

"I understand." Actually I was disappointed. I'd hoped to be able to send something hot upstairs to Corinne.

"I, you know, just want to see how things, you know, shake out here."

"No problem. I do understand." And it was the truth. I'd even been surprised in the first place that a guy making the kind of money he had to be making would even consider going through with it.

"I'll talk to you more about it. As I say, I've got nine chapters. But"—he hesitated, then gave a weak little laugh when he went on—"I've also got two more kids to send to college. And suddenly that's all that's in my head."

"That's not at all hard to understand. But whenever you want I'll be happy to look at what you've got."

"Great. And, look, I'm not sorry about bringing you up here and I hope you aren't either. I mean . . . about the speeches. I think you've got a real shot here."

"I hope so. We'll see."

"Look, we're going to stay in touch," Featherman said. It sounded almost like a plea.

"We sure will. You take care."

He walked me to his door and we shook hands. His was clammy and cold.

I went down to the fifth floor to try to make up with Stu Atkins. The section of the floor that housed the general promotion department gave off almost an echo of hollowness as soon as I walked in. Most of the L-units and offices were still empty after the "massacre." A secretary pointed to Stu's office—he'd had an L-unit when I was there—and I was surprised to see MANAGER over his door. I still couldn't even account for why he over so many others was still here.

He looked up as I entered. Then he grinned and stood up. "What the hell was that all about?"

"What was what about?" I tried not to smile.

"Cut the shit. What's with you and the brass?"

"Oh, they insisted on lunch. What was a girl to do?"

"They insisted." He nodded.

"Actually, and this is the truth, Ed Featherman called me. Yesterday. We met at a bar after work and we had a pleasant couple of hours together."

"He called *you*." He sounded stunned.

"And he invited me over today, and I met the boys, and I may be getting some freelance work."

"I'll be goddamn. Ed Featherman." He almost breathed out the name. "Christ, you'll never know," he said, shaking his head. "When I told him about your calls, I don't remember ever seeing a guy so mad. And then you two end up

170

having drinks together. And he even treated, I bet."

"He treated."

"Well, you never know," he repeated. "My oh my. Ed Featherman," he said again, as though with a shake of his head.

I looked at him. "Anyway, I want to congratulate you."

"On wha—" Then he stopped. "Oh. Thanks." He looked out the side-glass at the floor. "It's pretty much a nothing department now, but we'll be back. That I promise. We'll be back."

I hated to leave that building. I hated to leave the people. And as I waited outside for the cab I'd called, I couldn't help think of other cabs and the rides to the airport and the first-class seats and even, one time, being the only one in the compartment to LA, and a whole bottle of champagne on my tray.

I climbed in, and the darkness in my mind seemed to shade the day.

I thought of freelance work I might get. But I thought mostly of the exec's words, "We'll see." Like, maybe I'd be called back.

I don't know where it began to change, but I have the feeling it was as we were entering the first of the downtown streets. That what had happened to me at Packer-Hill became too unreal. Unreal, not as a fantasy. But like something wrong.

Chapter Twenty-Nine

By the time my cab pulled up in front of Mallory & Mallory, much of the high was back. I didn't care that I was almost three-quarters of an hour late or that I would be walking into grayness or that sour eyes would probably be looking up at me from the desks as I walked by. But nobody, in fact, seemed to notice me, not even Mrs. Dwyer, who was typing away at her desk. But I should have remembered that that was her way, for soon after I sat down she was in the doorway, announcing, "Mr. Meehan was looking for you," as if nothing at all was wrong.

"Did he say what he wanted?"

"No."

I took a deep breath, then walked up to his office, expecting hell and arming myself to give it back. He watched from his desk as I came in.

I said, "You wanted to see me?"

"No."

"Mrs. Dwyer told me—"

But he had already turned away. I stood there a couple of moments longer, raging inside. I forced myself not to say anything, to just walk away. But the fucker had my heart pounding again. To come back from there—from *there,* just a twenty-minute ride away, but a world away—to this! I dropped down at my desk, barely noticing when Mrs. Dwyer came in quietly and put the late mail on my desk.

I sifted through it without giving a damn, not even at the

one from Dr. Wheeling, whom I'd written to, special delivery, about his World War II memoir. His answer was not only fast, but short.

I am not interested in financing my own book. Kindly return my manuscript to me.

I read it indifferently even though I didn't have one new thing to work on now. In fact I sort of enjoyed routing it to Meehan and tossing it on the out-tray. A few minutes later Troy Roper was in my doorway. With that big grin of his.

"See the newspaper this morning?"

"This got to be about someone's obituary. You wouldn't be so happy."

"Another UFO sighting, this one in Michigan. Old Sam would be having a grand time planning how to get there for a weekend."

"Well, if he's where he deserves to be he already knows what it's all about."

Roper's face immediately became solemn. "You might," he nodded, "be right."

I looked at the empty space he left, then tried to think of some makeshift work to keep me occupied. But my mind kept drifting back to what he'd said. I could picture Sam at this desk, with that map out, planning the shortest route, then calling his wife to see if she wanted to go, if she could be ready. Somehow, though I couldn't see her always wanting to go, I also couldn't see her not going.

But what this also did was jolt me into an awareness that I had put Sam out of my mind, that it had become easier not to think of him. And my mind, almost against my will, began churning about him again. About Mrs. Crestman's "crazy" call to him, and her letter thanking him for destroying whatever, and what seemed to be the stench of strange, convoluted financing of Crestman's book, and even his testing of that drug, whatever the hell they called it.

I could call that cop who'd been over that time—what was his name?—Orster, Detective Orster—and just put it in his lap for whatever it was worth. But I hesitated and then didn't, telling myself I'd see, I'd think about it; that it might only hurt innocent people unnecessarily—and not only cost me this job, no matter how stinking it was, but any chance of getting back with Packer-Hill.

Chapter Thirty

My phone didn't ring all that afternoon. But then I got a call about four o'clock. I thought it might be Tina, telling me if she would be coming over that evening, but it was my mother. I was a little surprised since it was only a few days since I'd spoken with her.

"I tried to reach you at your apartment yesterday," she apologized, "but it was busy whenever I called. And I was afraid it'd be the same tonight. Am I interrupting here?"

"No, this is fine. Is something wrong? Are you all right? Dad?"

"Everything's fine here. But . . ." She hesitated. "I had to call to see how you are. There was something in your voice . . . I don't know. It's been worrying me."

"Really?" My mother wasn't all that much of a worrier. "No, I'm okay, I'm fine."

"Tell me, how's the job?"

My mother, though she was a practical businesswoman, had such belief in the basic honesty of people that she would never consider an operator listening in. But, anyway, I'd long made it a policy of never complaining to them about anything.

"It's going well," I said. "It's okay. Tell me, how's the real estate business?"

"Right now"—she had no such constraints—"not the greatest. But we think it's going to take off."

"Good. You take care of yourself. And say hello to Dad."

Hanging up, I had to sit for a moment and think about it. That was so unlike her. Certainly rare: she'd never been big on showing psychic powers. I think I shook my head a little; I don't remember. But I do remember a fleeting thought: that it called back, ever so briefly, the warning witches of Macbeth.

Tina showed up at the apartment about an hour later than usual. Her eyes looked edged with weariness. She'd just come from the apartment of an elderly couple, both the husband and wife confined to wheelchairs, one fixed to portable oxygen, and she'd waited until the aide promised by their social worker showed up.

"It's very sad."

I looked at her, wondering how she was handling it.

"You know what?" she said then. "It really does something when they even just touch your hand to let you know what you mean to them. Or kiss you."

A little later, as we were preparing to go out for dinner, she said, "I never asked about your day. How'd it go?"

"In one word, weird. It was a weird day."

She frowned. "Tell me."

I told her about my experience at Packer-Hill, after which she looked at me puzzledly, then said with a smile, "But that's great, that's wonderful. I don't see what you mean by weird."

"Honey, I was one of the low men on the totem pole in that place, I was laid off, and now I'm suddenly sitting with the brass and it's Tom this and Pete that and Chuck how's the golf? And a guy I wrote a speech for two years ago and never heard from since suddenly thinks I'm the greatest writer in the world and wants me to do more."

"So?"

"So it was weird."

"Well, enjoy it. Come on. I'm proud of you."

"And this guy Featherman . . . Can I tell you something? Can I admit something?"

"No, you can't. Of course you can."

"I can understand him being so scared shitless. Just as I sure as hell have come to understand Sam."

"Oh Tom." She was looking at me.

"I hate to lay it on you, but I just wish to hell I could get another job. I've *got* to get another job."

"Well, I've got a great idea." She took one of my hands. "Oh, is it a great idea. Why don't you just fucking quit?"

I looked at her. She would have done just that, I imagined. Walked out and worried about it later. In a way, though, I'd always looked on her as much older in the sense of being more mature than I was.

"Yeah," I said, "and then what?"

"I'll support you until you get another job."

"Oh, I knew there was a string attached."

"Or until you get a job after the next one."

I laughed. "You are," I said, touching the tip of her nose, "something special."

"Just quit. Why don't you just quit?"

"Honey, I can't. Not yet. You know the story. The best chance I have of getting another editorial job is being in one. Believe me. And I'll do fine."

"I know you'll do fine. But I think you keep forgetting it."

"I'm gonna write it down. How can I forget if I write it down? Got a piece of paper?"

"I'll give you paper," and we laughed together.

I was in a good mood at dinner, and certainly going to bed with her next to me. We made love, an especially gentle kind of lovemaking, where we spoke to each other softly, during, until the words disappeared into quick and then longer gasps, and then into silence and sleep. But as had been happening now and then, I woke up in the dead of night, pulses racing as if I'd been running. Racing without my knowing why. My heart was going so fast that I had to sit up for a while. I settled back slowly. Tina was sleeping with her back to me. I put an arm around her and moved close against her. I loved the soft feel of her, her smell. But I still couldn't ease back into sleep.

I turned on my back and stared through the darkness at the ceiling. I felt so impotent—which seems such a strange word after our lovemaking—but it felt so true with just about everything and everyone else. There was Mrs. Crestman, who I wanted to kill for what she'd done to Tina; maybe, even, that's the nightmare I just had. And that fuck Meehan. And my whole job—I'd started off just about fearless there, worked it to where even el-presidento had visited me, but now just about the only thing that separated me from Sam, poor dead, dead Sam, was the business of my being alive.

I literally felt like Sam in that bed. And I even helped it along, like the tip of a tongue on an aching tooth. I was seeing myself in that place ten, fifteen years from now. I became—had become—the Sam who takes all the insults and jokes. I live there within myself, finding hope, if I find it at all, in strange places. The most important thing is don't lose your job, don't lose your job. And when some broad I'll never see again in my life says get rid of this for me, I get rid of it without telling anyone, not even my wife, my beloved wife. And if this, somehow, has something to do with my death, yes it may be because I know something I shouldn't. But, most of all, I die because I've kept it to myself.

Chapter Thirty-One

I wasn't Sam, I was never going to be Sam, and yet even as I vowed this I felt a growing worry the next day, sitting behind that desk without a single thing to do. I told myself screw it, let whatever happened happen. But soon I was walking down the hall to our library, a small room at the end of the floor and began going through piles of medical journals and papers, most of which had already been routed to me. Just about everything I sifted through looked promising, great, for a moment, then became lousy. I brought a few things back to my office, which I checked out of there on the honor system, and began going over them at my desk. After a while I could hear people moving about, and I looked at my watch and saw it was noon. I didn't feel like facing people at the elevator, or mingling on the street, or going through the hassle of finding a table at some goddamn restaurant. I kept reading, though I soon wished I'd brought in something I enjoyed.

It was only a little while before I reminded myself, with a quick, almost electric jolt, of you-know-who.

It was as though, with that, something opened up in me. I didn't give a good goddamn if it cost me my job here, I had to let Allie Crestman know I knew of her call to Sam—where it all, whatever had happened, seemed to have begun. But I thought about it half the afternoon before I did, so angry at myself that I didn't trust I'd even be coherent. And I wasn't even absolutely sure of what I wanted to say. All I knew was that I wanted to throw a kind of bomb at her and see how she reacted.

I watched my finger pick out her phone number.

A voice I assumed was a maid's said, "The Crestman residence."

"May I speak to Mrs. Crestman? This is Mr. Loberg. Tom Loberg."

She came on. She sounded stiff, formal. "What can I do for you?"

"Mrs. Crestman, I hate to bother you but I have a question. I hope you don't mind. This will just take a minute."

She waited.

"I was just going through the files. You know, Mr. Glennie's files. And I see something here that may have been overlooked. I see where your husband received a grant from the Janquin Foundation."

Quietly, "Yes. So?"

"I'm wondering if it wasn't a slip-up that it hasn't been mentioned in the proofs. I'm sure you've seen it often—you know, 'the author wishes to thank the such-and-such foundation for its support—' "

"No," she said quickly. "The doctor doesn't want that." It was still "the doctor."

"That's a shame. I think it adds a certain prestigious something to it."

"No, just let it go at that." Her voice had gone from cool to icy.

"Can I ask you something?" I took a breath. "Did the doctor ever apply for a grant from Packer-Hill, you know the drug—"

"No," she cut in quickly. "What—why do you ask that?"

"I'm just curious. After all this time I'm just beginning to really go through all of Mr. Glennie's papers. It looks like he saved every single scrap, but they're in such a mess it's hard making some of them out. But I'm sure I saw something about Packer—"

"I don't know what's in there, I have no idea what's all there, but it's wrong about Packer."

"Oh?" Christ, even Ed Featherman had admitted easily to this.

"It's wrong. It's absolutely wrong. Now I'm sorry but I've got to go."

"Well," I said, just as she was hanging up, "it was nice talking with you, Mrs. Crestman."

A couple of hours later Meehan called me on the intercom to come to his office. For one of the rare times he looked directly at me from his desk rather than half to the side or at the desk. He motioned with a thin hand for me to close the door. It seemed to be trembling slightly, from the anger that was obvious on his face.

"What grade did you go to?"

I didn't say anything. But my head was saying plenty to me: Christ, now you really are Samuel Glennie!

"Third? Fifth?"

I kept looking at him.

"To insult one of our clients? How dare you."

Oh, this was it. "I haven't insulted anyone, Mr. Meehan."

"He just called! About his wife!" He gestured at the phone. "Dr. Crestman! He's a liar? You telling me Dr. Crestman's a liar?"

"I didn't say he's a liar. I just said I never insulted his wife. I did speak with Mrs. Crestman but I don't see where I insulted her."

"You don't see, you don't see! Look, you know something? You're just about hanging on here, you know that?

181

You know that? A second-grader would know when he's just about hanging on."

"I guess I'm not that smart," I managed to say.

"Well, you don't have too much time to smarten up. You understand? You understand that much?"

I looked at him. My heart was slamming against my ribs. I had all kinds of things to say, but they were all in the line of go shit in your hat, and you can take this fucking job—But the bravado was gone and I was suddenly afraid that if I as much as opened my mouth they would all come flying out.

The back of his hand motioned me away now, and he turned to some mail on his desk. I kept standing there. My legs were literally quivering. I turned and opened the door and walked down the aisle, past the secretaries, the offices, the cubicles. Ahead was my own office, its door open, the opening awaiting me, and Mrs. Dwyer talking with a little smile on the phone. She shook her head that it wasn't for me, and I walked behind her to go into my office, where in a moment I would close the door and go to that desk and try to bury myself, hunched over, in an old proof or in a book—

I turned and headed back. I was, in a way, less caught up in the rage that I'd been in just moments before. Instead I felt a kind of clean, polished anger, where every thinking part of me was focused sharply and to a point. I walked through his open door and up to his desk. His eyes lifted as he sat bent over, and then his whole head rose.

"You are one ugly man," I said.

His head seemed to jerk a little.

"You take the weakest people and step all over them. You did it to Sam, God how you did it to Sam, and you've been doing it to me. You don't know how to treat a person with dignity, let alone kindness. You're a wretched, rotten human being. And I'm glad to be rid of you! Because I am rid of you! As of right now!"

I whirled and walked out the door and into the aisle, not realizing until then that the door had been open and my voice had carried. Secretaries were looking up at me from their desks, and a couple of the editors were staring out of their offices. One was Troy Roper, his mouth a little open. My face flushed a little, but I didn't care who heard what.

I said to Mrs. Dwyer, who was too far back on the floor to have heard, "I'm leaving this place," and she turned and looked at me as I went in the office. I began taking whatever belonged to me out of the drawers and putting them in large manila envelopes. I would call Mrs. Dwyer about shipping me the few things that were left.

When I was about to leave I said to her, "It's been great knowing you, it really has," and I took her hand while she stared at me incredulously. "Good luck to you and your family," and I walked to the elevator. I was almost out on the street when I remembered, and I set down the packages and went through the first floor to the president's office.

"Mr. Mallory's not in right now," his secretary said.

"Please tell him that Tom Loberg stopped by, would you? I'll be in touch with him."

I gathered up my things again and walked outside. I thought of Sam.

Mostly in his honor, since he wouldn't have done it himself, I took a cab. And, in a sense that was very real to me, I took him from there with me.

Chapter Thirty-Two

Looking back to that time, how often I stop myself from making the second call I was to make to Mrs. Crestman. Instead I take the receiver from my ear and set it down, or I go outside and go running, or Tina is there in the apartment and she talks me out of it. And the tremendous compulsion to call her simply passes, and the future is whatever else it would have turned out to be. A big part of me even knew it then, that I shouldn't do it. And in fact I did hold off, for a day.

I came back to the apartment in a high and just dumped the packages on the sofa. I had no regrets, only a feeling of joy; but then again I'd had this even when I'd been laid off from Packer-Hill, from a job I'd liked: a glow of freedom, though it hadn't lasted long.

I made a mental note to myself that I wanted to write to Corinne, in Trade, and also send a letter to Mr. Mallory. But there was no one else in that place, except for Mrs. Dwyer, I would miss or who would miss me. I did, however, want to get in touch with Sam's wife, just to let her know where I was if she ever wanted me.

She answered the phone.

"Oh Tom, how good of you to call."

"I just want you to know I'm not at Mallory's any more."

"Oh?" She sounded alarmed.

"No, I wasn't fired, I left there, I quit. I'd had it."

I heard a little gasp, which was followed immediately by: "I'm really happy for you. I want you to know that. I really am. And I just know in my heart it's going to turn out so much better for you."

"Thank you, I appreciate that. I just had that place, I really did. I'm at my apartment now. And I just want to make sure you have my number."

She took a moment to get a pen, then scribbled it down. Then she said, "Oh, I only wish Sam had been able to do that. He felt he couldn't, so I guess he couldn't, and he made the very best of it, but I only wish . . ."

She was silent for a few moments. Then, her voice a little brighter, "You know, the two girls and I are planning a trip. We'll be traveling around the country."

"That sounds great."

"We'll be—we'll be visiting a lot of places."

"Terrific. I hope you have a wonderful time."

"And—I'm sure Sam will be with us all the way. All the way."

"I'm sure of it too."

And I was sure, also, that the "places" they'd be visiting were sites.

The truth is, not all of my mind was on that conversation with Edith Glennie. I had started thinking of calling Mrs. Crestman again during the cab ride home, in part because I wanted to get back at her, but mostly to see what would happen, what her reaction might be to what I was going to say. But, instead, I called Tina's office.

I was sure she was out on calls, but I wanted so much to tell her; and was right, it would have to wait. I left a message and she got back to me about four-thirty.

I said, "Sweetheart, how you doing?"

"Good. You?"

"Well." I smiled, almost as if she were there. "Couldn't

wait to tell you. I quit."

"No, you're kidding."

"No, I ain't kidding. Serious."

"You mean you gave them notice, right?"

"What notice? I'm through. I gave Meehan a blast and I walked out."

"You just blasted him and walked out? Just like that?"

"You've got it."

"Oh my. Oh great."

"It's done. Fini. Over."

"Great. Great. You didn't, uh"—I could detect a smile as her voice lowered—"pee on his desk?"

"Goddamn, I knew I forgot something."

"Oh, I love it. No notice, anything. I love it."

"Oh, they're going to give me one hell of a great recommendation."

Her voice changed. "Are you worried about that?"

"You kidding? Naah. I'm happy."

"You'll see," she said. "All you'll have to do is explain the situation. And you're going to find a terrific job, something you really want, you'll really love."

"Right now I'm not giving it a thought."

"Oh, honey, I wish I was with you tonight." She'd made plans, I knew, to spend the night with one of her sisters.

"Well, we'll go out and celebrate tomorrow. Big time. Meanwhile . . . you know what I'm doing? I mean right now, with you."

"Uh . . ."

"A hug."

"Ah. I like that."

"Hey," I said after a moment, "don't you hug back?"

"I am, I am."

"Oh, I didn't feel it."

"How about . . . now?"

"Oh, I feel it. Much, much better. And you know what I'm doing now?"

"Let's see."

"I'm kissing you. Right—on—those—lips."

Neither of us spoke. Then she said, "Honey, I'm sorry, I gotta go. Someone needs my desk. I'll try to call you a little later. Oh, and it's great news, great news!"

"You just have yourself a good time."

"I love you," she said.

"Oh, do I love you."

The apartment, when I hung up, gradually became different in a sense, as though her presence had actually been here and gone. But I still had that glow of having left something poisonous. It wasn't long afterward that I found myself thinking of Mrs. Crestman again, and burning to make that call. And it was all intermingled with memories of Sam, whom I hadn't given a thought to for a while. But it no longer held the fantasy of having taken him with me. Rather it was as if I'd abandoned his murdered body there.

I woke in the morning to the jolt of having nothing to do. But, after the initial touch of alarm, it was good. I intended spending much of the day writing new resumés, maybe spreading my search out to the West Coast. I didn't feel like making breakfast, or going over to the drugstore—I didn't want to talk, yet, about my ex-job—and went to a coffee shop several blocks away, where I had a good breakfast while reading the morning paper.

Tina called soon after I came back, and she was as high about what I'd done as when I'd first told her. Then it must have been only fifteen minutes later when the phone rang again.

"Is this Mr. Loberg?" a woman asked.

"Yes, who's this?"

"I tried your office," she explained first, "and they gave me this number. Miss Patricks. I'm Mr. Crain's secretary, he'd like to speak with you. Hold on, please."

It was only a few seconds before he came on, but in that wisp of time I was struggling to remember a Mr. Crain, then remembered Peter Crain, executive v.p. of Packer-Hill.

"Tom." And I pictured him, tall and lean, with a shaved head, leaning back in a swivel chair. "Pete Crain. Hope this isn't a wrong time for you."

"No. No. Not all."

"It was good seeing you. Glad we had the opportunity to meet," though I couldn't remember saying more than five words to him. "Look, I was talking to Chuck. And he had some mighty good words to say about you."

"That's good to hear." I was just remembering, in my confusion, that Chuck was Chuck Olson.

"I asked him if he was using you right now and he said he intended to in a week or so, so I asked him if I could borrow you. Do you have time for a project?"

"Sure."

"I'm giving a talk in a couple of weeks—and to tell you the truth, it's not exactly to a friendly bunch. They have a lot of preconceived ideas about what we do, and what I want to do is go into the process of what it takes to put a product on the market."

"I understand. I know that well."

"I'm sure you do. Anyway, and I'll be frank with you, but you've got to keep this to yourself—I have a draft someone wrote, and it's really, it's really not good. And that's putting it mildly. What I'd like to do is send you a copy as well as a batch of materials. I'd like you to read it over, let me know what some of your thoughts are, and we can go from there."

"Fine."

"We can talk price then or now." He sounded indifferent.

"Later is fine. Let me read it and I'll get back to you."

"Fine. I'll send it by messenger. I'll put Miss Patricks on and she'll take your address."

"Thanks."

"Thank you. Glad I met you, Tom. Real glad."

When I set down the phone I felt such a rush that it was almost dizzying. And I was too grateful for the assignment to think, again, how weird.

Maybe if the package had come early that afternoon I wouldn't have made the call. I don't know. But as I waited for it, my mind kept flashing back to Sam and Mrs. Crestman, to the secret that linked the two of them, and could lead— where? The funding of the book we already knew about? Something about Crestman's work with Packer-Hill?

I sat for a while just looking at the phone. Then, in a kind of blood-rush, I dialed quickly. What I heard next was the Crestmans' home answering machine, which was the least I was hoping for. But it might do.

"This is the Crestmans," her voice announced. "We're not in at the moment but if you leave your name and phone number and a message . . ."

I gave, simply, this message: "Mrs. Crestman. I thought you would like to know that Mr. Glennie never did destroy it," and I hung up quietly.

And immediately felt dumb. Like I was a kid back on Halloween—Mischief Night. I almost expected the phone to let out a blast right away, to hear a raging voice.

But after a couple of hours, still nothing.

★ ★ ★ ★ ★

The package arrived a half hour before Tina did.

"See?" she said. Her arms were around me, she was looking up at my face. "Your luck has changed already."

"Ooh," I said, "but I miss my old job."

"You wanna get hit?" She looked at me with a smile, then we kissed. "Did you read the stuff?"

"Glanced at it. It shouldn't be all that hard to do. But I'll tell you, I read that speech he sent—it isn't all that bad."

"But it doesn't have your poetry."

"Oh boy." Then, "Christ, it's strange though."

"What?"

"How it's happened."

"Don't question it. Just accept it."

I kissed her, only longer, slower, then looking at her I said, "I did something, you're probably going to think I'm crazy."

"You did pee on his desk."

"No, I forgot to do that. Damn, I knew there was something. No. This is about the lady Crestman. I called her again."

She looked at me as I told her. Then she laughed. "That's not crazy, that's revenge."

"Well, I was also hoping to see what her reaction was. Well, you see what it is," and I nodded toward the silent phone.

"Oh . . . I say let's celebrate."

"Where's my tux?"

"Let's celebrate," she said again, quickly.

We walked to a seafood restaurant in the neighborhood, where we each had a couple of hardshell crabs, giant-size, with french fries and cole slaw and beer. We were there until about eight. As we walked into the apartment house, a middle-aged husband and wife who lived on the same floor were just leaving . We said hello to each other, and as I unlocked the door Tina said, "They've been going crazy trying to figure me out."

"So have I."

"Oh, you louse." She poked me on the arm, her lips firm.

"Don't ask me what I meant. I have no idea. It's the beer."

"Well, you're flagged, you know."

She walked in first, and just as I closed the door behind us the phone rang. I immediately thought: Mrs. Crestman or the doctor. I felt a little quickening in my chest as I went to it.

"It's me," Mrs. Crestman's voice said. "And let me tell you."

I looked over at Tina. She was standing there staring at me. My lips said: Mrs. Crestman. But it was as though she already knew, that she read it on my face.

"What I told Glennie—what I told him were all lies! All—all made up! But you want to know why I told him? I wanted to get even! With my husband! Why? I'll tell you why! I'll tell you why! He was fucking your beauty! He was fucking her, you know that?"

My whole body went cold.

"That little whore! That little two-bit Greek whore! That piece of shit! That whore! He was fucking her, fucking her, fucking her!"

And the phone went dead in my hands.

I couldn't put it down. I couldn't let go of it. And I couldn't look at Tina. And then when I did, all I could do was stare. And I stared. And she was staring back at me. Then, a look of agony transforming her face, she turned and strode quickly to the door. She had trouble opening it, but she did. And I made no move to stop her.

Chapter Thirty-Three

I could feel a craziness coming over me. For moments I just stood there with every fingertip against my head, as though trying to keep it from swelling. I looked at the door, wide open as she'd left it, just looked at it, telling myself fuck her, fuck her, then I sank onto the edge of a chair. I kept seeing her beautiful, beautiful face, but in the most obscene way now, with his ugly face, that bald, massive head. How could she— with him? Him? But how—and it was if sanity were trying to seep back into me—how did I know that bastard witch told me the truth? It could have been her final getting even! But then I thought of that call she'd made to Tina and how Tina almost crumpled in a chair in front of me, just took her abuse without a word. Why else? Or maybe—I was grasping at any- thing—she'd simply been frozen by the attack, by that woman's craziness. And maybe she'd run from here, knowing from my face what the call was about, and, worse, that I be- lieved it.

The apartment felt so empty. And a feeling of panic was beginning to sweep over me, as if I had to retrieve or even just try to understand something fast or never again. I went to the doorway, looked down the empty hall, then started walking to the front door, then faster. I ran down the steps, then in the direction of Tina's apartment. I buzzed her from the vesti- bule but got no reply. I kept buzzing, then went to the back and looked up and saw no light in either of her two windows. I began running again, this time to the park, lighted in the darkness and fairly busy, and ran along all of its paths, then out to the street. There I had to stop for breath, bent over and my hands down on my thighs, but then rose up and began running again. I didn't know what I'd do if I found her, if I would try to hold her or if I'd yell into her face, straining to hold my fists back. But I had to see her, be with her.

I ran up and down several streets, then back to her apartment. And this time, with a burst of relief, I saw a light, dim but a light, in one of her windows. But she didn't answer my buzzing. And I couldn't make myself leave. But after about fifteen minutes I began walking away, slowly and looking back, only to break into another run, this time to my apartment. I went through the still-open doorway straight to the phone and called her. But it just kept ringing.

I walked away, sat down, stood up, then started walking to it again. Only this time it rang before I reached it.

"Hello!" I'd half-yelled it even before I brought the phone to my mouth but all I got from the other end was silence.

"Hello! Hello?"

"I—it's me—" Mrs. Crestman! For seconds I almost couldn't grasp it. Her voice was barely audible.

"What do you want? What the hell do you want?"

Again silence, even longer this time. Then, "I—I want—I want to see you." She sounded drunk.

"What about? What do you want?"

"The—truth. Tell you—the truth. All . . ."

Then was I right? She'd lied! I said, "Well, tell me!"

"Tell you—everything."

"Then tell me!"

All I could hear now was the sound of her breathing.

I said, "Talk to me. Hello! Mrs. Crestman!"

But it was a moment or two before I realized she'd hung up.

I had her phone number but in my hurry and confusion I couldn't think where it was, and I quickly called Information. But when I tried the number the line was busy. I waited, staring down at the phone, then started to pick it up but gave it another minute. And it did ring. I grabbed it up.

"Mrs. Crestman!"

"Can . . . come here? Want to tell you."

"Where's your husband?"

"Tell you. Everything."

"Then tell me! Tell me now!"

"All . . . all right."

But instead she was gone again, and I had the sense of her with a drink in one hand, and the phone having slipped from the other. I set down the receiver, staring at it. Then I ran out of the apartment and over to the garage.

I had the eeriest feeling driving there, a feeling of fear; was being drawn there only by Tina, the truth about Tina. But I had no intention of simply walking into that house, not with that crazy, she could have a gun, a knife. But I wasn't just going for this mad drive, either. I had no idea what would determine if I as much as rang the bell of that house, but I wanted to look at it, to see.

I turned into that street of large, widely spaced homes and stopped at the foot of the driveway. I stared up at the white, porticoed house. The first floor was lighted, and one of the upstairs rooms was too. There were cars up on the driveway, floodlights bathing them.

I kept sitting there, staring. Then I got out and closed the door as much as it would close without making noise. I would leave my car out here in case, after a quiet approach, I changed my mind. I walked up the driveway. As I stood at the bottom of the steps I looked around. One of the two cars there was a Mercedes. I didn't know what the other was.

I took the first step, then stopped.

The Crestmans, I recalled from my one visit, had two Mercedes. That didn't mean anything unusual to me—until within seconds it did. It was like something only birds hear—or perhaps sense—that sends them abruptly soaring. I started to whirl around but a voice, a man's, said from the doorway, "Don't, don't, don't!" And my head shot up and the first thing I saw, though his hand partly concealed it, was a gun.

The second thing, holding it, was Edward Featherman.

He closed the door swiftly behind me, grimacing under that crewcut, and bizarre-looking, here with that gun, in bright plaid pants, white shoes and a yellow sport shirt. Mrs. Crestman was standing by the sofa, her skinny face tortured, her blond hair disheveled.

"I—I didn't want—I didn't—" she stammered to me. And then, to him, "Where is my husband?" she pleaded.

"Back!" He motioned us to another room. "There! Go!" Somehow, despite his tan, his face was red. Even his scalp seemed red through his crewcut.

"Where is my husband? Tell me."

He looked at us. His chest was pumping. His eyes looked moist. And suddenly, in the whirl of my thinking, I also had fragments of thoughts of those guys in the white shirts—I couldn't even remember names, I saw only shirts! They part of this?—them *too?*

"My husband—my husband told him," she began stammering to me. "About you—calling me, about you knowing. But he told him—told just—just to warn him. My husband—husband—didn't know—know he'd do this. He didn't know, I didn't know, that he—that he did Mr. Glennie."

"All right." Featherman looked to be trying to catch his breath. "All right. Shut up you stupid bitch, shut up!"

"I don't know anything!" I said to both of them. "I made it

up! Sam—Glennie did destroy it, whatever you told him to!"

"Oh God." She began crying. "Oh God." Then, "Listen." She was staring now, but at neither of us. It was as though she had to tell something to herself. "I told Mr. Glennie—I-I was mad at my husband, and I told Mr. Glennie about it—about the tests. The drug. That he didn't deserve any book, any honor. And I—I wrote it to him, even. But then I was sorry, and I told him—please, please get rid of it. And that's all I know. Oh God."

But I'd stopped looking at her. I swear I even—maybe just for seconds, but it's true—I stopped even thinking of the gun, who was holding it. It was as if my mind could contain only one horror at a time; that it was true about Tina and him!

"Where is my husband? Please? You didn't hurt him, tell me you didn't."

I stared at him, with vision that was almost blurred from helplessness and rage.

He should have been out on a golf course in that outfit. He should have been at a lawn party, with his scotch or martinis. He should have been quietly high and leering at a neighbor's wife. He should have been with the doctors, wandering among them and their wives, stopping to ask did they like that trip he'd set up for them and how are those golf clubs working out?

He raised the gun and shot Mrs. Crestman dead.

It happened fast, and yet in a way I saw it as a slow-motion movie, saw the hand come up as though by degrees, saw it seek out her face, heard the terrible noise. But it was as if there were spaces in which I could act. I flew forward to my knees, then up at him as he was raising the gun again. My head smashed into his midriff, and he fell backwards. I fell with him beneath me to the floor, my hands fighting for his gun hand. He suddenly began punching up at me, which meant he'd dropped the gun, and I dug my fingers into his face, his eyes. He whirled away from me and began scrambling away on his knees—I knew for the gun.

I leaped up and after an instant's decision ran to the door. I had hold of the knob, was turning it when the gun roared and the window near my head shattered. I flung the door open and jumped the steps, made an even faster decision whether to run to the car or the back. Though a moonless night, it was still too bright out there under the streetlights, but even as I was still debating it I was running to the back. I cut through what seemed in the blackness to be a garden, felt my way around a hedge, skirted a dark swimming pool—and then stopped.

I could hear movement somewhere back there in the darkness. I pressed myself down against the ground, then rose to one knee, ready to try to spring on him or take off. But I could hear nothing.

Then the air seemed filled with sound.

An engine had come alive on the Crestmans' driveway. Then a car zoomed away.

Chapter Thirty-Four

I ran up to the nearest house. It was big and dark except for a dim light I could see somewhere through a window. I rang the bell, then rang again. I began pounding a huge knocker on the door. Then I started to run to another house, the closest, about half a block up the street. But I couldn't get a response there either. I ran back to my car but didn't jump in. Instead I looked up the driveway at the Crestman home; I could see only one car now. I began walking up there, slowly at first, thinking crazily that maybe it was all a trick, that somehow he was still in there; then faster, with the sudden desperate hope, which I'd never had for an instant, that she might still be alive. The door, I saw, had been left flung open. I stepped in, careful not to touch anything, and then from the living room saw her still body on the floor, her bloody face turned toward me against her shoulder.

And almost at that moment I heard a police siren in the distance. Obviously someone behind those closed doors had called the police.

I ran out to the sidewalk, then gestured to a squad car that turned the far corner. As people began drifting toward us from their houses, a young officer looked up at me from the window.

"There's been a murder! He just drove away. And he's got a gun!"

"You knew who? And the car, the license?"

I quickly gave him Featherman's name and description.

"But I don't know the car, except it was black."

I also told him that Dr. Crestman, wherever he was, might be another victim.

I was taken to the district station house where of course I told them what I knew. The problem, though, was that Mrs. Crestman had been so nearly incoherent that I had to try to piece together what it all meant. Angry at her husband, she had told Sam something about the testing Dr. Crestman had been doing for Packer-Hill on their new drug, something that was wrong about it, and she'd followed it up with a letter. Then, regretting it, she asked Sam to destroy the letter, which he did. Despite his destroying it, though I didn't know any details, this apparently led to Featherman killing him. Then later when I pretended that Sam really hadn't destroyed the letter, Dr. Crestman had told Featherman about it, which then exploded into this night.

I never even hinted at why Mrs. Crestman had been enraged at her husband.

I got back to my apartment close to four in the morning. I just sprawled out on the sofa without opening it. I lay there, exhausted and eyes closed but still fully awake, feeling my heart beating up at me. After all I'd been through I was thinking only of Tina.

I didn't sleep more than three hours. And I woke to the loneliest feeling I've ever imagined one could have. I made myself coffee and drank it standing.

I'd been interviewed at the station house by newspaper and TV people, but then got a call from another one about ten that morning.

"I don't know if you know it or not," he said, "but they just found Featherman."

"Good." That's all I could think to say.

An officer had spotted him less than an hour ago parked by a vacant lot in a black BMW. The only thing the officer could see of him was his crewcut and yellow sport shirt. Featherman, seeing him approaching with gun drawn, put his own gun to his mouth. But his hand kept shaking with it, and after about a minute he withdrew it.

"I wonder if you have any other reaction," the reporter asked me.

"No. Just good. And relief."

"Oh, and I don't know whether you know this. But they found Dr. Crestman. He'd been shot to death in his office."

Featherman was brought in crying, I was told. He was brought in bent over, his face away from the cameras, hands locked behind him.

Although I have never believed this, he was to claim that he had always acted alone, from the time Dr. Crestman came to him with a certain story, to having any knowledge of the murder itself.

The story that came out was that Dr. Crestman had told him that he'd identified three deaths as being the result of LG272. Featherman said he'd never reported this to anyone else in the company. Though it was only Phase Two of the study, the hopes for the drug were so high and the company so shaky, Featherman claimed he was afraid it would lead to more mass firings and a takeover. Though he was sure the drug would eventually be exposed, his hope was that it could be delayed until one of their other drugs that was in development, which had gone through all phases successfully and was with the FDA, was out on the market.

When Dr. Crestman told him that his wife had revealed it all to Sam, he panicked. He drove to the Mallory & Mallory building, knowing Sam's description, and parked near the entrance but wasn't able to spot him among the people flowing out. This was on the Friday before the murder.

"I told myself a hundred times not to go back," he confessed to the police. "I even went out Saturday to my club and played golf, I tried to play golf. But Monday I went back. And though I pleaded with myself don't take a gun, I—I had the gun."

This time, he followed Sam in his car, trying to convince himself that he just wanted to talk to him, to see if Sam had told anyone else what he knew, and if not just let him go. When they got to a place where Sam was walking alone, Featherman pulled up to the curb and called to him.

"Mr. Glennie. Mr. Glennie."

Sam came over.

"I tried calling you at the office but I couldn't get through. I know this isn't the way but when can I talk to you about a manuscript? It's going to be a big one, I'm really giving it to the pharmaceutical industry."

Sam was at the window. "Just send it in to me."

"Where are you going now? Can I give you a lift?"

"No thanks. I'm just going to the train station. It's only a few blocks."

And that, Featherman said, is when he completely panicked.

"I pulled the gun," he told the police, "and told him get in, get in. He looked like he was going to run away and I said do and you're dead. He got in and I began driving, holding the gun on him."

He drove to the park. There he had Glennie tell him everything Mrs. Crestman had told him.

"He swore he hadn't told anyone else, that he never would," Feathermen went on. "He pleaded with me to believe him and I did believe him that he hadn't, but I was so panicky I didn't trust him he never would."

When it grew dark he made Sam get out, intending to shoot him, but Sam broke away. And Featherman, dropping his gun in the confusion, leaped on him and wrestled with him into the shallows of the water, where he managed to hold his thrashing head under.

What happened after that, when I pretended to Mrs. Crestman that Sam hadn't destroyed the letter, was pretty much what we already knew.

Although I understand that the police questioned executives of Packer-Hill, they could not shake Featherman's story that he'd been completely on his own, that, incredibly, only one doctor—Crestman—and himself had been involved in the conspiracy to keep silent about the drug. And though he freely admitted bringing Dr. Crestman's request for a grant to the attention of the Elizabeth and Warren Janquin Foundation, the Foundation claimed it had gone through the usual "track" in awarding it to him.

Ed Featherman, father of three, two still to go to college, a private pilot and golfer and a grinner but in his own way a more frightened man than Sam Glennie ever was, was to get a life sentence.

He had never, incidentally, written a single chapter about the pharmaceutical industry.

I wanted to call Tina—but I didn't for several days. Then I learned from the operator that the phone at her apartment was disconnected. I tried her agency, but heard that she was on leave for a week. I immediately called her parents' home.

"She's not here," her mother said.

I said, desperate, "Do you know when she will be?"

"No." Then, "She don't want to talk to you. Goodbye." And hung up.

I wanted to run out and drive up there. I wanted to park

outside that row house and wait no matter how long it took. But I didn't. Those images were back—they'd never gone— and I was having an even rougher time with them.

Then, perhaps four days later, my phone rang and her voice said, without introduction:

"I just want to say this. I'm not proud of anything. I was in a mess in my life, I had no faith in myself, he'd helped me, and that was it. I just wanted to tell you that. That and— and—what do you think I prayed for? What do you think? Goodbye, Tom."

I sat there with the phone long after she hung up.

Call back, I told myself, call her back. But I didn't. It was as though I were maimed, and just couldn't. Maybe maimed, as I see it today, by pride.

The publicity got me a job with a New York book publisher, where I worked for eight years, then I moved on to another house, an even larger one, where I have been editor-in-chief for the past eighteen years. Yes, of the trade division.

I haven't married. Lots of women but no marriage yet. And I deliberately use the word "yet."

LG272 never did come out in the market: all at once, as if a plug had been opened following the first news stories of the murder, came reports from other doctors of deaths due to the drug. Packer-Hill itself is gone; or, rather, lives on like a Jonah in the belly of another drug conglomerate. I still think of myself in that cafeteria with the "boys," first names flying around and suddenly being the hot writer just when I began looking into Featherman. And I think of Ed Featherman, serving his life away, perhaps even, ah, "secure" with his pension still coming in. His family, I understand, is still on the old company's health plan.

Mallory & Mallory has been gone too, for at least twelve years. I was back in the city a couple of times, and on one of those occasions I made a few-block turn to see it again. It looked just as gloomy on the outside but I had heard that a music publisher had taken it over, and I let myself imagine those dark floors filled with tunes. I don't consider myself particularly mean but the thought crossed my mind that if old Frederick Meehan was still alive, breathing other people's air, how nice it would be if he had a great-grandchild in his house playing their CDs loud.

I thought of Sam, of course, though it didn't take seeing the building to trigger thoughts of him. He'd slip into my mind, and still does, at the oddest times, that quiet, hulking man with the fears that ultimately killed him. I don't want him to leave my head forever; he's still important to me in a sad way. For a time I kept in contact with Edith Glennie but she's moved away and we haven't spoken to each other in several years now. On one of the last calls I made to her, she told me that Janie died. Maybe, I couldn't help thinking, that was the help that finally came from space.

And Tina. Tina.

I must tell you, and maybe I should have done it before, but I haven't used her real name. She's married and has children, and I wouldn't embarrass her. I never saw her again—except for the other day, in a way. I was flipping through one of the entertainment magazines at a friend's house when my heart almost leaped from my chest. I was staring at her face, a much older face of course but with the same long hair, the same beautiful thin features, the same smile. She was with her teenage son, who has made quite a name for himself in TV. The article was mostly about him, but a little about her and her husband, a lawyer, and how successfully they raised their children.

I kept staring at the picture. How often I'd wondered what she looked like, what she was doing now, if she was having a good life. In fact I doubt if there's been a day when at some time or other I haven't thought of her. And it's always with regret. She had given what I look back on as a boy a man's feelings, and I think how much more she would have given to the man. Yet I often wonder too: how would I have lived with it? Would I have placed it in its place? I don't know. But I would have known, wouldn't I? I would have known.

2493